"The Lily Field" by Lenora Worth

Mariel thought this man was different from the corporate types she was used to.

Heath worked with flowers, for crying out loud! And he did look like a character from a historical romance novel. Intrigued, Mariel gave him a sharp stare. "So what were you doing standing out in the middle of the lily field?" she asked.

"I was listening to the lilies."

Okay, I've got a live one here, Mariel said to herself.

"The Butterfly Garden"
by Gail Gaymer Martin

Emily pictured the butterflies flitting among her flowers and she yearned for the past.

She wanted to enjoy her garden again and be free like those fragile creatures. Her eyes shifted from the lovely banners to Greg, and she caught him looking back at her. A mixture of embarrassment and pleasure spiraled through her chest.

Emily drew in a deep breath of the pungent spring air. As if the day were blessed, sunshine had turned the sky a gorgeous cerulean blue and heated the budding flower beds. New growth. New life. New hope

W9-AVY-039

LENORA WORTH

grew up in a small Georgia town and decided in the fourth grade that she wanted to be a writer. But first she married her high school sweetheart, later settling with her husband and daughter in Shreveport, Louisiana. After the birth of her second child, a boy, she decided to pursue her dream of writing full-time. In 1993 Lenora's hard work and determination finally paid off with that first sale.

"I never gave up, and I believe my faith in God helped get me through the rough times when I doubted myself," Lenora says. "Each time I start a new book I say a prayer, asking God to give me the strength and direction to put the words to paper. That's why I'm so thrilled to be a part of Steeple Hill's Love Inspired line, where I can combine my faith in God with my love of romance. It's the best combination."

GAIL GAYMER MARTIN

lives with her real-life hero in Lathrup Village, Michigan. Growing up in nearby Madison Heights, Gail wrote poems and stories as a child and progressed to writing programs for her church. When she retired, she tried her hand at her dream—writing novels.

An award-winning novelist, Gail is multipublished in nonfiction and fiction. Her Steeple Hill Love Inspired romance *Upon A Midnight Clear* won a Holt Medallion in 2001 and was a National Readers Choice Award finalist. Besides writing, Gail sings with a well-known Christian Detroit chorus and enjoys public speaking and presenting writers' workshops. Visit her Web site at www.gailmartin.com. She loves to hear from her readers. Write to her on the Internet at gail@gailmartin.com, or at P.O. Box 760063, Lathrup Village, MI 48076, U.S.A.

EASTER BLESSINGS

LENORA WORTH AND GAIL GAYMER MARTIN

Love Inspired

Published by Steeple Hill Books™

STEEPLE HILL BOOKS

Steeple
Hill™

ISBN 0-373-87209-7

EASTER BLESSINGS

Copyright © 2003 by Steeple Hill Books, Fribourg, Switzerland

THE LILY FIELD
Copyright © 2003 by Lenora H. Nazworth

THE BUTTERFLY GARDEN
Copyright © 2003 by Gail Gaymer Martin

Printed in U.S.A.

CONTENTS

Dear Reader,

Easter blessings! This time of the church year is so important to all of us as we celebrate our greatest gift— the death and resurrection of our Savior, who gave His life for us. We are both thrilled to be a part of this two-in-one book from Steeple Hill Love Inspired.

I've enjoyed writing with my friend Gail Martin. Together we wish all of our readers a blessed Easter. One of my favorite parts of this holiday is the Easter lilies. They are so beautiful and they smell so wonderful.

In "The Lily Field," Heath knew that the natural lilies growing in the field were far more precious than those that had to be forced in a greenhouse. Yet he also understood the importance of those forced lilies to the people who would buy them. Mariel was like a forced lily in that she wasn't ready to blossom. When she realized the Lord had been watching over her even in her darkest hours, she knew she could experience something just as precious and wonderful as a lily blooming in the field. On to you, Gail…

When Lenora and I agreed to do this book, my first thought was the butterfly, the symbol of rebirth, for my story. They visit my flower garden, and my home is decorated with them—in wallpaper, stained glass, on pillows and throw covers. But the concept of rebirth has a more personal meaning for me. A few years ago I experienced what Emily did in "The Butterfly Garden." My knees had been damaged by osteoarthritis, and after spending a few months in a wheelchair, I underwent two knee replacements. I thank God for the technology that allowed me to walk again without pain. This story of trust in God is a blessing to me, and I hope it has been for you.

We hope you have a happy spring filled with butterflies and lilies. And God's redeeming love. And until next time, may the angels watch over you—always.

Lenora Worth   *Gail Gaymer Martin*

THE LILY FIELD
Lenora Worth

To my sister-in-law, Kathy Baker.

Consider the lilies, how they grow: they neither toil
nor spin; and yet I say to you, even Solomon in all
his glory was not arrayed like one of these.
                                            —*Luke* 12:27

Chapter One

She saw him standing in the lily field.

Mariel Evans lifted a hand to her eyes, shading them from the bright springtime Louisiana sun, then blinked just to make sure she wasn't imagining things.

The tall man was still there among the rich green of the lily stalks. He stood with his back to her, hands on his hips, in a lightweight plaid flannel shirt and faded jeans, his dark blond shaggy hair gleaming with sun-washed shimmers as he surveyed the rows and rows of almost-budding Easter lilies.

Mariel stood at the edge of the field, afraid to move. The man seemed so deep in thought, she didn't want to disturb him. Glancing around, she wondered where her grandmother was, wondered why exactly she'd been summoned here to White Hill in the first place.

She'd parked around front, then when she couldn't find anyone at the house, she'd walked down the meandering lane past the gift shop and nursery, past the rows of greenhouses, heading toward the fields. Only to find them deserted, too.

Except for him.

She glanced back toward the man. And he turned to look right into her eyes.

The beauty and intensity of his classic, chiseled features stopped Mariel in her tracks, leaving her awestruck with wonder while her heartbeat accelerated. He looked like a proud lion standing watch over his domain, his nostrils flaring with awareness as he lifted his head. That awareness, that alert attention, only made her *more* aware of him. And made her a bit nervous, too.

Get a grip, Mariel silently told herself. But that advice was hard to take, considering the way the man stood there assessing her with a head-to-toe look. Deciding to take matters into her own hands, she advanced toward him, ignoring her suddenly breathless state. "Hi. I'm Mariel Evans. I'm looking for my grandmother, Sadie Hillsboro."

The man moved toward her, a slow, lazy stride that showcased his long, muscular legs. When he got about two feet away, he tipped his head sideways, causing his longish hair to fall across his eyes. "Hello. Sadie told me you'd be arriving today." He extended a hand. "I'm Heath Whitaker, the new manager."

"Oh, hi," Mariel said, her gaze locking with his. She was immediately taken again, this time by exotic, slanted eyes so deeply blue and sparkling, they reminded her of a 3:00 a.m. sky. She took the hand he offered, her fingers tingling from the warmth of his firm grip. "Granny mentioned she'd hired a new manager."

"That's me," he said, his smile soft and tight-lipped. "*Granny's* mentioned her favorite granddaughter a time or two to me, too."

Mariel let go of his hand, then tossed her long chestnut-colored hair off her face. "I'm the oldest of her five grandchildren. I've had more time to work my charm on her."

"She thinks highly of you," he replied. "Always bragging about how smart you are, how you paint these pretty pictures on computers—graphic art, I believe?''

"That's my job." Mariel glanced around again. "Where is she, anyway?"

"She's at the doctor," Heath said, touching her arm to guide her back to the wooden white house up on the hill.

Alarm coursed through Mariel. "Is she sick?"

Heath nodded. "Your grandmother hasn't been well lately at all. We had to convince her to go in for a checkup. Dizzy spells, fatigue, no appetite. Your two uncles had a time getting her to go."

"She can be pretty stubborn," Mariel said as they walked up the gravel-covered lane, the vanilla-like scent of lilies wafting through the air after them. "Is that why she called me to come home?"

"Partly," he said, pushing a hand through his thick hair. "I'll let her explain everything to you when she gets back." Then he stopped, his work boots crunching against pebbles. "So you're here for a long stay?"

"About a month," Mariel replied, worry making her impatient. "I took a leave from my job in Dallas." At his questioning look, she added, "I had some comp time coming anyway, and Granny sounded so firm in her request…. Well, let's just say I thought it was a good time for a vacation. She never mentioned she was in bad health, though."

Heath nodded. "You know your grandmother. She's proud and tough, just keeps on keeping on."

"*You* sure seem to know her very well." That he did bothered Mariel for some unnamed reason. After all, this man was a stranger.

"I've been here since last fall. Hired on at a very crucial time, right when the lily bulbs had to be transferred into the greenhouses for the Easter schedule. Been working hard at it since, but I do take a minute here and there to visit with Sadie. After all, this is *her* bulb farm.''

''She knows everything there is to know about growing Easter lilies, that's for sure,'' Mariel said, her gaze lifting toward the rambling white Victorian house that she'd come to love over the years. ''White Hill is famous for its lilies.''

Heath nodded. ''Tell me something I don't know. That's exactly why I signed on here in the first place. And I've worked in Oregon and California, even in Del Norte County.'' He paused, as if waiting for Mariel to acknowledge this information.

Since she didn't understand the significance, she lifted her brows. ''I take it Del Norte County should mean something to me?''

He grinned, shook his head. ''It's the Easter Lily Capital of the world,'' he explained. ''You don't have a clue about Easter lilies, do you?''

''Not even a smidgen,'' she admitted. ''I spent summers here with Granny and worked in the fields and the store, but all I really remember or know is that the field we were just in is the original White Hill Easter lily field, started with a few bulbs my grandfather gave her long ago, right after he came home from World War II.''

Heath nodded. ''She loves to tell that story. Highly romantic, don't you think?''

Mariel *thought* this man was different from the corporate types she was used to being around. He worked with flowers, for crying out loud! And he did look like a character from a historical romance novel.

In answer to his question, she laughed. ''My grandmother has always been a romantic at heart.''

''But you're not?''

She shrugged. ''I'm too practical for hearts and flowers.''

He made a little noise that sounded suspiciously like a grunt. "We've got our work cut out for us, then."

"What on earth are you talking about?"

"I'll let Sadie explain."

Confused, but intrigued, Mariel gave him a sharp stare. "So what were you doing standing out in the middle of the lily field?"

"I was listening to the lilies."

Okay, I've got a live one here, Mariel thought. He was probably one of those tree-hugging nature lovers—after all, he'd said he'd lived in Oregon and California.

"So…part of your job is to, uh, listen to the lilies?"

Heath's eyes went a shade darker, as if he knew she was teasing him. "Yes. You see, I *love* that field. Do you know it's one of the only naturally growing lily fields in this country, maybe in the world for that matter, other than the wild lilies on some tropical island somewhere? I mean, all those beautiful lilies got there strictly from propagation—and your grandmother's loving hands, of course."

"Of course."

"We're lucky we have a late Easter this year," he said, waving a hand. "Normally, we don't get many bloomers in this field until May. But this year…I just have a good feeling that we'll see some blooms on Easter morning." He shrugged, gave her a sheepish grin. "This field can't be rushed or forced, you know?"

Mariel studied his features. He was so earnest, so intense, so…nice looking. Mentally shaking herself out of her stupor, she looked back down the lane toward the main field.

"I only know this. When those flowers start blooming, so white and pure, the scent makes me think of an exotic island somewhere far away." She felt the childhood memories rising up, but pushed them back to a safe distance. "I love that field, too," she said, surprising herself by the admission. "When I was a little girl, I used to run through the rows, pretending it was my wedding chapel. The blooms would be over my head…and the smell—" Realizing she'd been rambling, she shut up.

"Like no other perfume in the world." Heath finished, amazement in his eyes, that soft smile on his face. "You *do* feel it, too, then?"

Shocked, Mariel shook her head. "Feel what?"

"The power of the lilies." He lifted a hand in the air. "The power of God's beauty."

"I don't know about God," Mariel replied, flushed with awareness and hugely embarrassed by having shared some of her most treasured memories with this handsome stranger, "but I think one of the reasons Granny lets that particular field grow wild is because it reminds her of how much she loved my grandfather. It brings her so much comfort. And I guess, yes, I felt something running through those rows as a child. It brought me comfort so many times."

"That's what I'm telling you," he said, taking her by the arm to lead her up onto the wide wraparound porch. "Easter lilies bring people joy and peace. They represent what faith is all about—being reborn, being resurrected through God's grace. When you stand in that field, you can feel that. That's why I love growing lilies." He took a breath. "And that's why I love *listening* to the lilies."

"I believe you," Mariel said, thinking this man took his job way too seriously. "No wonder Granny hired you."

"What's that supposed to mean?"

"Oh, nothing. Just that…my grandmother is a very devout woman. She lives by faith. And apparently, so do you."

"Don't you?"

"I—I just live," she replied, a trace of bitterness in the statement. "One day at a time."

"So you don't see the joy?"

"What kind of question is that?"

"Simple enough," he said as he leaned back on a porch railing carved with intricate grape leaf designs and curlicues.

"I have…joy," Mariel said on a defensive lilt, wondering why his sure, steady gaze made her want to squirm away. Maybe because he seemed so direct and honest, two things she'd never mastered. "I'm relatively happy with life."

"Okay."

"Okay." She whirled to go inside. "I guess I'll go unpack while I wait for Granny to get home. Do you want to come in?"

He heaved off the rail. "No. I've got things to do. Another couple of weeks and we'll be real busy around here, shipping out the hothouse lilies."

"Then I won't keep you," Mariel said, glad to be getting away from him. "It was nice to met you, Heath."

"You, too," he said with a grin. "I'll probably see you for supper." He shrugged. "Sadie likes to make sure I get at least one hot meal a day."

Mariel watched as he took the steps two at a time. Probably in a hurry to get back to…listening. "I'll see you later, then."

He turned on the tulip-lined path. "I'm sure we'll be seeing a lot of each other around here. That'd be nice." Then he gave her that soft smile again.

Mariel leaned back against the door frame, then brought a hand to her heart. "That one's different," she mumbled to herself. And so very interesting. Where on earth had her grandmother found him?

"Granny, what are you up to?" she wondered aloud as she headed into the cool darkness of the big house. "And why was it so urgent for me to come home?"

She had a sneaking suspicion Heath Whitaker had something to do with all of this. And as soon as her grandmother got back, Mariel intended to find out just exactly what was going on around here.

Chapter Two

"Granny, are you sure you're up to having company for supper?"

Sadie Hillsboro turned away from the red beans and rice bubbling on the stove, her wrinkled hand reaching for Mariel. In a cultured Southern drawl, she said, "Child, Heath is not company. He's like family to me. Now stop fussing and come sit at the table so we can have a nice chat before we eat."

Mariel took her grandmother's hand, then sat down on one of the old chrome-backed kitchen chairs. "Are you sure about him? I mean, he seems to be good at his job. He obviously knows all about growing lilies, but—"

"But—" Sadie smiled, her pink-rouged lips parting as she pushed a hand through the soft white tuft of hair piled in a bun on top of her head. "Do you find Heath a bit intense, dear?"

"That's putting it mildly," Mariel replied, memories of Heath's compelling eyes making her blush all over again. "He's not like the men I know."

Sadie kept the smile on her face as she fingered the

ancient strand of pearls hanging in a long loop down the front of her lace blouse. "You mean he's not like...let's see, what's his name?"

"Simon," Mariel said, holding a breath as she waited for a stern lecture from her lovable grandmother on love and marriage. But the lecture didn't come.

Instead Sadie sat back against her chair, her eyes—the same shade of green as Mariel's—contemplating her granddaughter. "No, Heath is not like that Simon fellow you keep mentioning in your letters and calls. Heath understands things such as commitment and values. He comes from good stock—his whole family has worked the lily fields in California and Oregon for close to seventy-five years now. Three generations of farmers, you know."

Mariel would have rather had the lecture. But instead, she got a glowing report on White Hill's new star manager. Mariel once again got the impression that Sadie and Heath were in on a secret. She wanted to know what that secret was.

"Heath's record sounds impressive," she said, treading lightly so her sharp-as-a-tack grandmother wouldn't clam up. "How did you find him?"

"The Internet, of course," Sadie said with a flutter of her long lashes. "After our Dutch decided to retire—you know he's getting on up in years now—I posted a Help Wanted ad on our Web site, the one you designed for us, and we just love it. Soon I had prospects coming in from all over the country." She paused, waved a hand in the air. "'Course, none of them could live up to Dutch Ulmer. Until we saw Heath's résumé. Somehow, I just knew it was right. So I prayed about it, read the Bible, and do you know what happened?"

"No, Granny. What happened?"

"I decided the way I always decide. I shut my eyes,

flipped through the Good Book and pointed to a random passage.''

"Really?'' Amazed at how her grandmother has always made major life decisions in this way, Mariel could only shake her head. She certainly didn't hold any stock in consulting an ancient tome on what to do with her life. That little voice in her head suggested maybe she should give it a try, since her current practical methods didn't seem to be working, but Mariel ignored that. "And what verse did you land on, Granny?''

Sadie's face beamed with a light of pure contentment. "Luke Twelve, Verse Twenty-seven. 'Consider the lilies of the field, how they grow.' You know the passage, of course, don't you, Mariel?''

"Of course,'' Mariel replied. She no longer read the Bible, but she sure remembered her grandmother quoting that particular passage often enough. It had always been a favorite of her grandmother's, for obvious reasons, Mariel thought with amusement.

Sadie clapped her hands together. "It all made sense to me then.''

"So you hired Heath, based on that verse?''

"Oh, no,'' Sadie said, shaking her head. "I went out into the big field first—this was way back late last summer, so there weren't many blooms left, but I stood there, listening to the lilies. Then I came in and called Heath right away.''

Mariel let out a groan, then got up to butter the French bread. "Does everyone around here listen to flowers?''

Sadie stared hard at her granddaughter. "Why, yes, I reckon we do. It's part of our job. Do you find that offensive?''

"I find it rather odd,'' Mariel replied as she slammed the bread tray into the oven. "I guess I don't get it.''

"You used to 'get it,''' Sadie replied, "and it's my firm

hope that one day you will remember that.'' She patted Mariel on the back. ''And that's part of the reason I asked you to come for this visit.''

Mariel turned to hug her grandmother close. ''Well, I'm glad I'm here, what with you having these health problems. I'm worried about you, Granny. You have to listen to your doctors. A bad heart is serious.''

Sadie gave Mariel a tight squeeze, then stood back to smile up at her. ''My heart is just old, honey. And tired. But I'm going to behave and follow the doctor's advice. I'll be fine. I have to stay strong until I've accomplished the things I have yet to do.''

Mariel wondered what things her grandmother meant. All afternoon, Sadie had been tight-lipped about what she expected now that Mariel was home. They'd talk at supper, was all she could get out of Sadie. That and the doctor's warning that Sadie was headed for a heart attack if she didn't slow down and watch her diet. The doctor wanted to do some more tests, but Sadie had refused.

Mariel's mission for now was to make sure Sadie followed through, whether her grandmother liked it or not.

Sadie, however, seemed perkier than ever tonight. ''Your uncles are coming, by the way. They can't wait to see you.''

''I'd like to see them, too,'' Mariel said. ''But I have to wonder why they don't check on you more often.''

''They're busy with their jobs,'' Sadie said with a shrug. ''Family things—soccer, Little League, Junior League, PTA meetings, the usual.''

Mariel didn't mention that they only lived a few miles away and could easily drive to White Hill on any given day. Instead, she broached another sensitive subject. ''Have you heard from Mom lately?''

Sadie's bright eyes seemed to fade out a bit. ''Not since Christmas. Your mother does her own thing, I'm afraid.

Always has, and always will.'' Then she looked at Mariel. ''What about you? Have you talked to her recently?''

''I called her to tell her I was coming here for a few weeks, but I could never reach her. I wanted her to know where I'd be in case she needed me.''

''Your mother doesn't need people,'' Sadie replied on a sad note. ''Or at least that's what she'd like us to believe.''

Mariel had long ago given up on trying to figure out her mother, Evelyn. Her parents had divorced when Mariel was ten, and none of them had seen her wayward father since. Evelyn, once a vibrant, pretty woman, was now a bitter middle-aged shrew who blamed everyone and everything for her troubles. Mariel tried to keep in touch with her mother, but Evelyn's tendency to criticize and whine had turned Mariel off too many times to keep them close. Her mother lived in Florida, and rarely visited the tiny town in northwest Louisiana where she'd grown up. White Hill held too many painful memories, Evelyn had told her.

Mariel wondered now if that was why she didn't come to White Hill too often herself. In spite of the many hours of happy times she'd spent here, it had been here that she'd found out about her parents' divorce. Maybe her mother was right. Some memories were just too painful.

The screen door opened with a swish, bringing Mariel out of her bittersweet memories.

She looked up to find Heath Whitaker standing there in a clean blue shirt and fresh jeans, his eyes centered on her.

''Hi,'' he said. Then he shoved a dainty bouquet of trailing honeysuckle into her hands. ''These grow along the fence behind my cottage. Thought you and Sadie might enjoy them.''

Mariel took the flowers, savoring the sweet smell of the delicate yellow and white blossoms as she held them to her nose. ''Thanks.''

Sadie dropped the big spoon she'd been using to stir the rice, then wiped her hands on her ruffled white apron. "Heath, come on in. Supper's just about ready. Iced tea or water with lemon?"

"Tea would be nice," Heath said, his eyes still on Mariel. "As long as it's sweet."

"Granny only makes it that way—half sugar, half tea and water, I believe. She'll need to cut back on that some now that the doctor's put her on a healthier diet."

Mariel whirled to find a vase, acutely aware that both her grandmother and Heath were watching her. And from the smug look on her dear grandmother's face, Mariel got the distinct impression she'd been set up.

Her grandmother was playing matchmaker. That must be why she'd asked Mariel to come here. Sadie wanted her first-born granddaughter to find true love and happiness, the way she had with Grandfather Jonas.

Mariel had certainly heard Sadie express that wish for her often enough. Sadie didn't think Mariel could truly be happy with Simon what's-his-name back in Dallas.

And lately, Mariel had begun to suspect her wise grandmother might be accurate on that account. She and Simon were definitely on the outs right now.

She turned and gave a shaky smile to Heath Whitaker, deciding as matchmaking went, however, he wasn't a bad choice.

Not bad at all. But that didn't mean she was ready to get involved with a man who listened to lilies and picked her honeysuckle straight off the fence. Mariel had no intention of acting on her overly romantic grandmother's obviously misguided ploy to bring Mariel and Heath together.

No intention at all.

But then Heath smiled back at her. And brought all of

her carefully controlled defenses crashing down like an out-of-control mudslide.

I'm in serious trouble here, Mariel thought to herself.

The other two people in the room kept right on smiling at her.

Serious trouble.

Chapter Three

They made it through supper without too much embarrassment, if Mariel didn't count the way her grandmother kept smiling back and forth between her and Heath Whitaker, like the cat that had swallowed the cream. Thankfully, before Granny could drop any more obvious hints, her uncles arrived in time for dessert and coffee.

"Let's go into the living room," Sadie suggested. Mariel took a tray laden with coffee cups and a decanter in and set it on the round polished Queen Anne coffee table. Her grandmother followed with a steaming pan of peach cobbler, and Heath followed with dishes and spoons.

"Where's the ice cream?" Uncle Kirby said, winking at Mariel.

"Didn't get any," his mother replied. "Besides, I have to get the low-fat kind now. Just didn't seem the same, if you ask me."

"Now, Mama," Uncle Adam said, taking the bubbling peach cobbler from her to place on a pot holder, "you'd better heed Dr. Kirkland's advice. You have to eat right and exercise more."

"Do I look overweight to you, son?" Sadie asked, her hands on her hips.

Mariel had to smile at that. Her grandmother was so petite, she seemed like a little doll. "It's not your weight, Granny. It's your cholesterol. That's the culprit. You're just too good of a cook."

"I can attest to that," Heath said as he poured coffee for everyone. "I think I've gained five pounds since I came here."

Mariel's uncles laughed. They seemed to like Heath as much as Granny. Mariel wanted to like the man, too. She just hadn't figured out what was so special about him. Besides listening to lilies and such.

Once they'd all settled onto the ancient Victorian sofa and chairs, Mariel's uncles grew quiet and waited for her grandmother to speak. Mariel looked from one to the other, wondering what was going on. Then she looked over at Heath. He just gave her that little half smile, then turned his gaze back to Sadie.

"Y'all ready?" Sadie asked. When her two sons nodded, she let out a sigh then smiled at Mariel. "Honey, we're all real glad you could take some time off to come to the farm. As you know, we get busy around here this time of year. Spring is on the way, and we've got to start shipping the lilies we've been nurturing in the greenhouses."

"I understand, Granny," Mariel replied. "Do you need my help? Is that why you insisted I come immediately?"

"Well, yes, and no," Sadie said, pausing to take a long sip of her decaf. "Mariel, we asked you here for a very important reason. And before you say no, I want you to listen very closely to what I'm telling you."

"Granny, you're scaring me."

"Nothing to be scared about," Uncle Kirby said, his plump hands folded in his lap.

"Let me just tell her," Sadie said, her tone firm but soft. "Mariel, as you know, your uncles have good careers in the city. Kirby is an executive at one of the largest banks in Louisiana. And Adam is president of his own construction firm. They stay busy with their obligations and their families."

"Yes, but—"

Sadie held up a hand. "Hear me out, please. Long ago, these two worked hard here on the farm. But neither of them wanted to stay here at White Hill. I sent them both off to college down in Baton Rouge, and they got to see some of the world. So I didn't begrudge each of them their desire to live and work in Shreveport. However, I had hoped one of them might come home someday, to take over the farm."

"You'd think," Mariel said, looking at both her uncles. They each squirmed and shifted their feet. She turned back to her grandmother. "So, is that what's happening now? Is one of you going to take over the farm now that Granny's sick?"

Kirby cleared his throat and adjusted his tie, his gray-tinged hair glistening as he shook his head. "Delores and the kids like living in the city, I'm afraid. I can't do it."

Then Adam shook his head. "And Bree feels the same way. Kids are in good schools, got a great set of friends, a good church. I just can't see forcing them to move back out here, miles away from everything they've come to know."

"I see," Mariel replied, thinking she could at least understand that. She liked living in Dallas and she had her own career there. "So what's the plan?"

"You, dear," Sadie said, her green eyes centering on Mariel. "I asked you here because I've made a decision, and the boys have agreed with me on this decision."

Mariel stared over at the "boys," both of whom continued to squirm. "What's the plan, Granny?"

"I'm leaving the farm to you," Sadie blurted out. "After I'm gone, I expect you to carry on the tradition of growing White Hill Easter lilies."

Mariel shot out of her chair. "Hold on a minute! You're telling me Uncle Kirby and Uncle Adam have agreed to this? What about their inheritance, what about their children? What are you talking about, Granny?"

"You'd have controlling interest," Kirby, the banker, explained. "You get twenty-six point five percent and the land and the house. We—meaning your mother and us two—each get twenty-four and a half percent and any profits from that. And our children would inherit that from us, while you would inherit the remainder of your mother's holdings."

Mariel felt the heat rising on her skin. "So you're telling me I could inherit the bulk of this place, lock, stock and barrel, and you'd both just sit back and rake in whatever profits are to be divided between us?" When everyone nodded, she threw a hand in the air. "Why are we discussing this? Granny, you're sick but not anywhere near death." Then she stopped, her heart slamming into her chest. "Oh, Granny, you aren't dying, are you?"

"Not anytime soon, I can assure you," her grandmother said on a dry note. "I'm just getting my affairs in order, is all. And after many long hours of discussion with the boys, I've decided this is the best solution. You see, dear, they wanted me to sell the farm and move to one of those fancy retirement villages back in the city. I'd just as soon swat flies off a donkey's tail."

Mariel saw the amusement on Heath's face. It infuriated her. "And just where do *you* fit in with this plan?"

"Me?" Heath pointed to his chest, then tossed his sun-streaked bangs out of his face. "I get to train you, to teach you how to grow lilies. And how to *listen* to lilies, too."

Mariel pivoted to stare into the empty fireplace. "That is ridiculous. I mean, why can't you two just oversee things for Granny? Why can't you help her out?"

"We've been helping her out all along," Kirby explained. "We keep up with her taxes, her finances, any type of business concerns she might have. We just can't come out here and physically run the place. That's why we suggested she might consider selling after Dutch decided to retire. Dutch ran this place, with Mama overlooking things and working by his side, but Dutch got old. We just suggested selling out as the best option."

"But she's not having any of that," Adam said. "So we have to abide by her wishes."

"That's right," Sadie said, getting up to come and touch Mariel's arm. "And it is my sincerest wish to have *you* home and running this farm. You'd be perfect for the job, Mariel. You know these lilies. You practically grew up here as a child, and I've seen you out there in the big field. You have the heart and the head for this."

Mariel turned to find all of them staring at her, three with hope, and one in particular with skepticism. "I have a career, too. And I have a life back in Dallas. You're asking me to just walk away from that?"

"Only after I'm gone, if you want to wait until then," Sadie said, her statement as calm as if she were offering up more cobbler. "Of course, I was hoping you'd just start in the near future."

"I don't even want to have this discussion," Mariel replied. "What about Mother? Doesn't she get a say in this?"

"Over the years, your mother has refused to discuss it— said she didn't want any part of this old farm. I haven't told her about this plan, but I won't cut her out of her inheritance, no matter how stubborn she is.''

The hurt in Sadie's words made Mariel stop and take a calming breath. "Well, at least she will have an interest. Maybe if I tell her that, she'll come home and talk about it.''

"That's up to you," Sadie replied. "I'm done with her for now.''

"Why me, Granny?''

"Well, I can't wait until the other four grandchildren are grown. You're the oldest. And I told you, you have the heart for it.''

"And we don't," Kirby said. "We grew up here and we love this old place, but life goes on and we have our own lives now. It would be a burden—''

"A burden?" Mariel's anger stopped him short. "A burden? This place is the only Easter lily farm in all of Louisiana. They said it couldn't be done, that the climate wouldn't support growing lilies, but Granny proved all of them wrong. She made this *old place* a household name all across the South. A White Hill Easter Lily is of the finest quality. I can't imagine an Easter without lilies. A burden—''

This time, the hand on her arm wasn't her grandmother's. It was Heath's. "I thought you didn't know much about lilies.''

The admiration in his eyes was unsettling. "I don't. I mean, I know enough. And I know that…we can't sell this place.''

"Then you're my only hope," Sadie said, pride in the words. "And…I only ask that you stay here through Easter, let Heath teach you. If after that time, you don't think you want to do this…then I'll eventually make plans to sell the farm and move to town.''

Mariel looked up at Heath. He smiled, nodded, then

dropped his hand from her shoulder. "Sadie, I think you've found the right person for the job, after all."

"You had doubts?" Sadie said, a spark of amusement in her eyes.

"A few."

"But not anymore?" Mariel asked, wondering what kind of doubts he still had about her.

"I'm beginning to see the wisdom in this plan," he said. Then he leaned close. "And the challenge."

"What do you mean by that?"

"Oh, like I said earlier, we've got our work cut out for us."

"Just because I don't listen to lilies?"

"No, just because you don't listen to your heart. But there's hope."

"What would you know about my heart?"

"Not much. But you just stood here and fiercely defended this place, so I'm looking forward to learning a whole lot more."

Mariel glared at him, then became aware that the room had grown quiet. Her uncles and her grandmother were all watching her expectantly.

With a frustrated sigh, she said, "I'm here through Easter anyway. Might as well see what this place is all about. But I'm not making any decisions or promises. I have a good job and…responsibilities of my own."

Even as she said the words, she realized she had nothing. Nada. There wasn't really anything holding her in Dallas. She could do her graphic design and Web site work from just about anywhere. And Simon… Well, they hadn't exactly parted on the best of terms.

"Of course, dear," Sadie said, uncommonly docile for the moment, in spite of the glee in her eyes. "So when do you want to get started?"

Mariel turned back to Heath. "I guess I'll be reporting for work bright and early tomorrow morning."

Heath took a sip of coffee, set the cup down, then waved good-night. "Like I said, I'll look forward to it."

Mariel watched him walk away, her whole being telling her this was a very bad idea. Her grandmother hadn't brought her here for matchmaking. She'd brought her here for keeps.

Only, Mariel wasn't sure if she was disappointed by that, or afraid to think ahead to what the next month would be like.

Then it hit her—maybe Granny had a dual purpose in mind. Maybe she wanted Mariel to work with Heath in hopes that she would fall for him.

And want to stay here with him for longer than a month.

Mariel remembered the image of Heath standing in the middle of the lily field, and for just an instant, she thought she heard a long sweet sigh moving on the wind.

Then she realized the sigh had come from her.

Chapter Four

This time, she found him in the greenhouse.

He was once again engrossed in his work. The rows and rows of lilies in green plastic pots had two-inch buds, some of them turning the whitish hue that indicated they were ready to open. Heath was measuring a bud, his expression serious as he hunched over his work.

It was chilly in the greenhouse, a cool sixty-five degrees to keep the lilies happy. It didn't make Mariel happy. She shivered a greeting. "Hello, Heath."

He whirled, that bemused smile on his face. The smile annoyed Mariel. It was just too early in the morning for him to be so...perky. And to look so good.

"Did you get breakfast?" he asked as he moved down the long row toward her.

"Coffee," she replied, stifling a yawn. "What about you?"

"Not yet. I came out to check the lilies first." Then he moved past her, the swish of his jeans echoing down the long, narrow walk. "Come on. I have a pot of coffee and some cinnamon rolls Sadie gave me yesterday. I'm willing to share.''

Confused, Mariel hurried to catch up with him. "I thought we were going to work."

"We are. Over coffee."

He didn't elaborate, so Mariel had no choice but to follow him. "Where is this coffee and food?"

"My place."

He held the door open for her. Mariel stepped out into the bright dawning sun, the scent of lilies following her. Several of the other workers were arriving, starting their busy day. She could their voices echoing through the gardens. "Oh, and where is your place?"

"I'm living in the caretaker's cottage," he said as he pointed on down the lane, past the big lily field.

"That old place!" Surprised, Mariel shook her head. "Dutch didn't live there. Why are you?"

"I'm not Dutch," he retorted as he strolled along.

"You can say that again."

"Hmm?"

"Oh, nothing. Dutch lives in—"

"I know where he lives. He has a nice brick home on the other side of the property." Heath stopped to wait for her, his hands on his hips. "But I saw the cottage, and decided I liked it. So Sadie and I struck up a deal. She said I could live there rent-free if I'd be willing to do some renovations on the old place."

Mariel tossed her long ponytail. "Yeah, well, that doesn't surprise me. You two seem to be good at striking up deals."

That brought a frown to Heath's usually serene face. "If you don't want to do this, just tell me now. I don't like wasting my time."

Surprised by the snap in his words, Mariel wanted to tell him he didn't have to waste his precious time on her, but she needed a bit more caffeine to fortify her. And her stomach was growling rudely. "Can we discuss this over that coffee you promised me?"

The smile was back. "Sure. Right this way."

They walked past the lily field in silence, the lemony-vanilla scent from a thousand near-budding blossoms assaulting them. Mariel heard the bees humming, heard the wind whipping through the tall pines beyond the field, and she understood the peace this place could bring to a person.

It was good to be back here.

Except for him.

She glanced over at Heath. He was looking ahead, his features set as if he were in deep thought.

Probably thinking about how best to "train" me, she told herself. Just to show herself, and maybe him, that she *was* trainable, she stopped and tried really hard to listen to the lilies. She closed her eyes, held her head back and waited.

She wasn't sure what she was waiting for or what she was supposed to hear, but she wouldn't let this interloper get the best of her.

Not on an empty stomach, anyway.

Heath watched Mariel as she stood there among the lily stalks. When she lifted her head, her eyes shut and her full lips parted, he felt a hard punch right to his gut.

She was a pretty woman. He'd have to be blind not to notice that right away. Long auburn hair, exotic green eyes. And lots of attitude.

When he'd looked up to see her standing there yesterday, something had fluttered inside his chest, something soft and lovely, like the wings of a butterfly. Now as he watched her, he could understand why Sadie had insisted on bringing her granddaughter home.

Mariel Evans looked as if she belonged here. She wore baggy denim capri pants that showed off her long legs and a loose-fitting, faded blue sweatshirt that made her look like a tomboy. But she was definitely all girl.

"What are you doing?" Heath asked, the question more for himself than her. He wanted to know what she was doing to *him*. He didn't usually let things distract him. And he never let *people* distract him.

She kept her eyes closed, her head lifted. "I'm trying to listen to the lilies."

He grinned at that, then stepped close enough to get a whiff of her hair. It smelled just about as good as the flowers. "And what do you hear?"

Mariel's eyes flew open in surprise. "Don't sneak up on me like that!"

"What? I just walked over to you. And you didn't answer my question."

She gave him a frown. "I don't hear anything except the wind in the trees and a few hungry bees buzzing around. I think some of the stalks rustled at me, but that's about it."

"You're hopeless."

"Yes, I am. Which is why I don't like this notion of me taking over the farm. Bad idea, very bad."

He turned away. "Come on. We need to talk."

She followed him in silence. When they reached the tiny white cottage, he heard her gasp. "You really have been doing some renovating."

Heath looked up at the newly whitewashed house. "I'm rather pleased with it myself. Sadie showed me pictures of how it used to look."

Mariel touched a hand to one of the carved porch posts. "This is where she and Grandpa Jonas first lived. Just them in this tiny little house. They were so happy."

Heath nodded, enjoying the way her expression turned

all dreamy. "Sadie told me all about it. Told me how they built the big house after the boys came along."

"Yes, a few years after the war. Jonas worked the land and Granny raised the boys and my mom, and tended her gardens."

"And grew the first of the original White Hill lilies from the ones Jonas brought back after the war."

She glanced at him, her green eyes reminding him of the first tenders sprouts of a baby bulb. "Yes. Her little flower bed turned into this field. They just kept growing and growing through propagation. People would come for miles to buy bulbs from her." She looked down then, her eyes sad. "Then Grandpa Jonas had a heart attack and died, right there on the front porch of the big house just a few years after they'd finished building it."

"He was so young," Heath said. "He never saw his fortieth birthday."

"You have been talking to Granny."

"Does that bother you?"

"No, why should that bother me? You need to know the history of this place, I guess, if you're going to stay here for long."

Heath stared at her, saw the challenge in her words. "Is that what this is all about? You don't think I'll stay here and see this through?"

Mariel walked past him up onto the porch. "I don't know what you're talking about."

Heath hopped up onto the porch beside her, then placed a hand across one of the shutters he'd just painted a light yellow. Leaning into the shutter, he asked, "Are you afraid I won't fulfill my end of this deal? That I won't stay here on the farm and help your grandmother?"

"Does anyone really stay anywhere anymore?" she asked, the words bursting out of her mouth.

"Do I detect a bit of bitterness there?"

Her eyes seemed to turn to fire. "Look, let's just stick to the lilies, okay? I don't need analyzing or training, and I certainly don't need you trying to figure me out."

Heath pushed his hand off the window shutter, then held it up in surrender. "First of all, I'm here to stay. I fell in love with this place the minute I came up the driveway. And second, I think I could really enjoy analyzing you, but unfortunately, we don't have time for that. So, I agree. Let's get to work. Now quit pouting and come inside and have some coffee."

"I don't like you," she said, her voice calm and crisp in spite of the scalding look she gave him.

"Well, you don't have to *like* me," he replied, stung by the bluntness of her words. "You just have to work with me for a month, until you can fully understand how to grow lilies."

She followed him into the house, her gaze scanning the small sitting room and the long, narrow kitchen. He'd worked hard to refurbish this place, mostly with castoffs from Sadie's attic and a few treasures he'd found at flea markets. He dared her to say anything about his haphazard decorating scheme.

She didn't. Instead she said, "I don't want to grow lilies."

"Sadie thinks you do."

"Well, I think this is unnecessary. Granny is just worried because she's sick. But if she listens to her doctors, she should be around a very long time."

Heath poured two cups of coffee, then placed them on the old white wooden table he'd found in the barn out back. "Sit."

Mariel glared at him, but she sat down, her expression full of concern. "Just how sick is my grandmother?"

Heath sat down next to her, then offered her a cinnamon roll he'd just warmed in the small microwave sitting on the counter. "She's not telling the whole tale. She's fainted a couple of times. Last time it happened, Dutch and I thought she'd had a heart attack." He took a sip of coffee, watched her face for a reaction. "The doctors say it's angina."

"She'll be seventy-six her next birthday," Mariel said in a quiet voice. "That's hard to believe."

"Well, believe it," Heath replied. "Look, Mariel, I came here last fall for a job. I've worked hard all my life, and all that time, I've worked with my hands out in the fields and dirt. It's what I do. My dad passed away about two years ago and my mother moved from California back to Kansas to be near her sisters. I got restless, so I decided to travel. But that got old pretty fast. So I looked for a job, and I found this one. I had the experience, and coming here gave me a new challenge. It's been great so far."

"Thanks for the history of Heath Whitaker." She nibbled her roll, then asked, "Why is it so great here? I mean, I love this place, but why do you?"

He relaxed back against the squeaky wooden chair. "It's peaceful. It's…Godly here."

"Godly?" She laughed out loud.

"You have a problem with godly?"

"No, I just don't base much on how godly a place is."

"Obviously, since you live in Dallas."

"Hey, I like Dallas—we've got the Cowboys, both the football team and real-life cowboys, we've got the Rangers for baseball, the Galleria, the Reunion Arena—"

"And traffic nightmares and smog and…crowds."

"I don't mind all those things."

"I don't mean to knock your city," he said, trying to form the right words. "After all, I did live in California for most of my life. But don't you ever get tired of all of it? I mean, the hassles, the overcrowded freeways, the constant waiting for the next light to change."

"Sometimes," she said, her eyes centered on her breakfast. "But what does that have to do with God?"

"God is here," Heath tried to explain. "He's out there in that lily field. He's given your family a tremendous blessing. Easter lilies represent everything there is about Christ—being reborn, the resurrection, forgiving, living."

"Wow, you're really into this stuff."

Heath smiled. "It's not just stuff to me. It's what I believe. It's what my parents taught me and it's what your grandmother lives by. And that's one of the main reasons I like it here."

"I know. And I don't mean to knock religion. I've just never put it first in my life."

"Well, here you can do that."

"Maybe I don't need to do that."

Heath shook his head. "I don't know about you, Mariel."

"I don't know about you, either, Heath."

"Well, we're stuck with each other for the next few weeks, at least."

"Yep. Maybe we shouldn't discuss religion."

"Or politics?"

"Or anything, except lilies, of course," she said, but she smiled when she said it. Then she surprised him. "Oh, and by the way, I love what you've done with the place."

Chapter Five

The sun was setting off to the west. It had been a long, busy day and Mariel was tired down to her very bones. But a sense of contentment settled over her as she sat down on the gray-painted porch steps to stare out over the horizon. The barns and outbuildings glistened a golden-white against the sun's last burst of rays. The lilies stood tall in the field, reminding her of a green river, their white buds like flowers floating on water. And down the hill, she could just see the shape of the tiny cottage where Heath had made a home.

Home.

This had to be one of the loveliest spots on earth, she thought as memories of her first day at work played through her mind.

She had told Heath Whitaker she didn't like him, but that wasn't exactly the truth. She was intrigued by him, no doubt. And he was a very nice man. So what *didn't* she like about him?

Maybe the way he made her feel—part giddy, part wary,

and completely, very much aware that he was a handsome man and she was a confused woman.

She'd watched him with the other workers. Where Mariel lacked patience, Heath was patient to the point of being annoying. He took the time to explain to her each step of the intricate process of growing commercial Easter lilies, from checking for waterlogged soil, to making sure the baby plants in the back fields weren't infected with spider mites or the roots weren't being eaten by hungry gophers and armadillos while they went through their three-year rotation. The workers, both men and women alike, seemed to respect Heath. And he worked as hard as any one of them.

Mariel had watched him as he moved through each greenhouse, giving instructions about fertilization and pruning, checking the delicate buds to make sure they were healthy and pest-free. The lilies had to be perfect.

The forced flowers would be shipped out to florists, nurseries and retail outlets over the next couple of weeks. By the time consumers bought them and gave them to loved ones, or left them on graves in celebration and memory, their blooms would be completely open.

And Heath seemed determined to make sure White Hill was shipping the very best. At least he understood that about this place.

White Hill set very high standards.

That was a challenge, just as he'd told her this morning. That challenge scared Mariel while it enticed her, much in the same way Heath both scared and enticed her. Because Mariel set high standards, too. Maybe that was why she felt so conflicted when it came to Heath.

What if he didn't live up to her standards?

Or worse, what if *she* let her grandmother and him down?

"What am I doing here?" she mumbled, her dirt-stained hands dangling over her bent knees.

"Looks like you're waiting for supper," a deep, chuckling voice said from the corner of the house.

"Dutch!" Mariel jumped up to hug the jovial man who'd been like a grandfather to her.

Dutch Ulmer grabbed Mariel and lifted her a foot off the ground in a bear hug that took her breath away. Then he dropped her back down, a wide grin splitting the wrinkled crevices of his aged face. "Look at you, girl. I declare, ain't you a sight for sore eyes!"

"You, too, old man," Mariel teased, her own smile hiding the "happy" tears—as Sadie would say—misting in her eyes. "So you finally decided to retire—maybe do some of that fishing on Caddo Lake you've always talked about?"

"Yes'm," Dutch said, taking off his faded LSU ball cap to rub a hand over what was left of his once-red hair. "I reckon I can go fishing or courting or whatever else I set my mind to."

Mariel laughed. "Then what are you doing here?"

Dutch rubbed his rounded belly. "Your granny asked me up to supper, to see how things are going with you and this new fellow. I been out of town—went down to New Orleans to visit my sister. How are things going?"

Leave it to Dutch to get right to the heart of the matter, Mariel thought. He was around the same age as her grandmother, but he'd never married, and everyone knew he'd carried a torch for Sadie for close to four decades. Everyone that was, but Sadie. She considered Dutch to be a good friend and a trusted manager. Sadie refused to look beyond that.

Mariel had to wonder if she didn't have a lot of Sadie in her, since she refused to think of Heath Whitaker in any terms other than co-worker and manager.

"Things are going," she said in answer to Dutch's question. "I think Heath is a good replacement—he can never fill your shoes, of course, but he's a hard worker and he knows all there is to know about lilies."

"I can't argue with that," Dutch said, nodding his head, his gray-tinged red whiskers glistening in the sunset. "I wasn't sure at first, but your granny, she has such good instincts about these things, I had to listen to her."

"She consulted the Bible, as usual," Mariel said as they walked up the steps together.

"Whatever works," Dutch replied, grinning. "Ain't never failed her yet."

Before they went into the house, Mariel lowered her voice. "Dutch, I'm worried about her. She's finally listening to the doctors about her health, but I'm afraid she might have waited too long."

Dutch bobbed his head, his watery blue eyes brightening. "We all tried to tell her. Stubborn woman, that one. Glad y'all got her to the doctor, at least."

"You can thank Heath for that," Mariel said, that touch of resentment settling over her in spite of her gratitude to Heath. "I think he and my grandmother have bonded."

"That's good, that's good," Dutch said, a knowing grin on his face. "You don't cotton to that, do you?"

"Am I that obvious?" Mariel said, her voice still low. "I guess I'm just worried. I mean this scheme to get me here to possibly take over the farm—it seems as if Granny is trying to run my life, and that's not like her. I don't like being shoved toward a man I don't even know."

"Is that what she's doing?"

"I think so. Why else would she summon me here? I think she's matchmaking under the guise of having me take over the farm."

"Maybe she's killing two birds with one stone."

At his snicker, Mariel only shook her head. "I don't

know what's going on. And I don't know enough about Heath to form an opinion one way or another on either his managing methods or his personal assumptions regarding me."

Except that my heart does a double beat each time the man looks at me.

"If it's right, you'll know enough," Dutch said as he opened the screen door then bowed with a great flourish, his hat in his hand. "And remember, your grandmother is a very wise woman." He winked. "After you, young lady."

Mariel entered the cool, dark hallway, resolve making her spine stiffen. No use to whine to Dutch. He was on the other side already. He'd always be loyal to her grandmother, so Mariel couldn't hope to have an ally in him. Not that this was a battle. It wasn't. She could tell them this was all ridiculous and just leave whenever she got ready.

That shouldn't be too difficult.

But when she walked into the kitchen to find Heath there laughing with her grandmother, her treacherous heart admitted what her head didn't want to hear. It would be very hard to leave White Hill now.

Now that she'd spent a whole day following Heath around. Now that she'd realized she really did like him.

A lot.

Heath liked being around Mariel. A lot. And that surprised him. A lot.

They'd worked together side by side, her asking questions, him giving her precise, clinical answers. But there was nothing precise or clinical about how she made him feel. That was more like warm and fuzzy and confused.

He knew as little about her now as he did this morning. She didn't allow for much personal information. So far, he'd learned that she enjoyed her work in computer graphics but had needed this few weeks of downtime—why?— that she had a small apartment just outside Dallas and that she loved her grandmother enough to indulge Sadie while Mariel was visiting. Beyond that, Heath had found very few details about the real Mariel Evans.

Heath had always prided himself on the details.

Growing lilies was all in the details. Everything had to be calculated, based on the calendar, based on when Easter would fall. The details had to be worked out months ahead of time, and an accurate timetable had to be followed. Once that was in place, the details moved to the actual growing process, the staggering of the bulbs from babies to mature plants to forced blossoms in a greenhouse.

Details and timing. His world revolved around those two things.

Now, when he looked up to find Mariel laughing and smiling with Dutch, the details flew out the window and he had to wonder if his timing was a bit off.

She looked adorable with dirt smeared across her face and mud caked on her capri pants.

Adorable did not fit into the details.

"Hello," she said, her eyes on her grandmother. "Look who I found lurking around the porch."

"Dutch," Sadie exclaimed, clapping her hands together. "I'm glad you're home from New Orleans. How was your trip?"

Dutch rolled his eyes. "Mardi Gras—bah! Me, I can live without that 'throw me something, Mister' baloney. One big party. I told my sister to get me out of that crazy city."

"You didn't enjoy carnival?" Heath asked, his eyes following Mariel.

"Not one bit," Dutch said, his eyes on Sadie. "Didn't want to even go to a parade, but my nieces and nephews thought I'd get a kick out of it. After five minutes, I'd had enough. Missed my little house and my little garden. And peace and quiet. Glad to be home.''

''Well, come on in and wash up,'' Sadie said, turning back to the stove. ''I've baked a ham and there's potato salad in the refrigerator. We'll have ham sandwiches for lunch the rest of the week.''

''Granny, you don't have to cook so much every night,'' Mariel said. ''I can cook for us.''

Sadie chuckled. ''Honey, we don't eat that low-fat frozen cuisine around here.''

''Well, you have to start,'' Mariel pointed out. ''Ham isn't good for your arteries.''

''It's lean, and I'm only going to have a sliver,'' Sadie replied. ''And I made the potato salad with all low-fat ingredients and plenty of green peppers and onions, just as the dietitian suggested. And I made a fruit salad for dessert. Does that meet your approval?''

''Yes,'' Mariel replied through a yawn.

Heath gave her a thumbs-up, then grinned. ''Are you tired?''

''Tired and sore. Granny, I'm going to get a quick shower and change, then I'll set the table.''

''Okay. Should be ready in about twenty minutes.''

Mariel whirled, glanced at Heath, then left the room.

Dutch and Heath both turned to Sadie. ''Fruit salad?''

''It's ambrosia,'' Sadie replied smugly. ''With marsh-mallows and coconut. But I did use low-fat sour cream.''

''If you made it, I'm eating it,'' Dutch said with a tip of the head.

Heath saw the love in the other man's eyes. Dutch was hopelessly devoted to Sadie Hillsboro. What was in the air around this place? Maybe because it was springtime, everyone was getting all mushy around here. Anyway, he decided, there was a lot more going on at White Hill than just growing lilies.

A whole lot more.

When Mariel emerged about fifteen minutes later, washed and wearing a long pink cotton T-shirt dress, and smelling like a garden, Heath vowed to stick to work. Stay the course. Follow the plan.

Only, sometimes, God had other plans. He wondered if that was why Sadie wanted Mariel and him to work together.

Was there a future for them in Sadie's plan? In God's plan?

For once, Heath didn't have the details laid out before him. He couldn't calculate this situation.

He smiled at Mariel, but his heart beat a fast tempo, a tempo that didn't give him any answers. Then he remembered what his father had always told him.

God was in the details, too.

Heath would just have to let nature take its course and see how the next few weeks played out. Mariel had wondered if he had staying power.

Now Heath wondered the very same thing about her.

Chapter Six

"**I**'m glad you decided to stay for a while," Sadie said.

Mariel held her grandmother's arm as they strolled down the gravel lane toward the big field. Sadie wanted to see the lilies up close.

"Me, too," Mariel admitted. She'd been here for a week now and she had to admit, she was sleeping better and she felt better over all. "I've been burning the midnight oil for so long, I'd forgotten to stop and rest."

"And to stop and smell the lilies," Sadie said, patting Mariel's arm. "You look rested. So Heath isn't working you too hard?"

Ah, Mariel had wondered when they'd get around to the subject of Heath Whitaker. "Not really. I'm used to hard work. But this work is different. It's interesting and it keeps me busy."

"Interesting enough for you to accept my proposition?"

"Granny, I'm just not sure I feel comfortable, knowing that if…something happens to you, this place would suddenly be my responsibility."

Sadie stopped as they reached the outskirts of the big field. "Let's go sit on my bench."

Mariel guided her to the old wooden bench perched across the wide lane, underneath a towering live oak that had been there for two centuries. The secluded spot gave a perfect view of the sloping field.

It was late afternoon. The day had been warm, but now the gloaming had arrived. Mariel could feel the cool drafts from the nearby woods. "Are you cold?"

"No, dear, I'm fine. Just right." Sadie straightened the skirt of her dress, then turned to Mariel. "You need to understand something, darling. I picked you for the job because I know I can trust you. I've always favored you over my other grandchildren."

"Granny—"

"Now, before you go getting all worked up, hear me out. The boys know how I feel and they don't begrudge me that favoritism, because you are the firstborn. They know I love them and my other grandchildren, but honestly, those citified teenagers of theirs don't give two hoots about this old farm. They only come to visit when their parents force them out here. So we have an understanding. I won't bother them about being all lovey-dovey, if they won't tell me what to do with my land and property. It works for me."

Mariel shook her head. "But it shouldn't have to be that way. Your grandchildren need to learn respect, and they need to understand that this 'old farm' gave their parents a good, solid start in life."

"They wouldn't get it," Sadie replied, a stubborn set to her lips. But Mariel saw the hurt in her grandmother's expression, too.

"Maybe we should clue them in," she said quietly.

Sadie sighed, her gaze moving over the flowing lily rows. "Maybe. But there is one more very important reason I want you to consider this.'' She turned to Mariel then, her expression softening. ''It's your mother.''

''Mother? What's she got to do with this?''

''Everything,'' Sadie said. ''I don't know where I went wrong with Evelyn. I loved her just as much as I loved the boys, spoiled her at times, at other times held firm against her rebellion. I tried to teach her values as any mother would, but we've just never seen anything eye-to-eye.''

Mariel shifted on the bench. ''So you're willing me the farm to appease my mother?''

''No, I didn't say anything about appeasing anyone. It's a solid business decision, based on prayer and careful reflection. But I am hoping that if you inherit this place, maybe move back here to run it, it will bring your mother home. Even if I'm not here to see it happen.''

Mariel stared at her grandmother, an outpouring of love pooling inside her heart. Sadie was a devout woman, a woman who believed in the power of God's healing grace. It was so like her to think of others instead of herself. So like her to still love and care about the daughter who had turned her back on her family long ago.

Obviously, Sadie had thought about this for a long time. And obviously, she thought this was the only way to bring a sense of healing to her family. If Mariel moved back to White Hill, eventually Evelyn would have to come home to visit. And Sadie was hoping that would begin to heal the rift that had developed between Evelyn and her family years ago. In her own gentle, loving way, her grandmother was offering her more than a lily farm. She was offering Mariel a legacy that would sustain the generations. And bring her mother back home.

''What if Mother doesn't agree to this?'' Mariel asked now. ''What if she resents you for...this manipulation?''

"Do you think I'm trying to manipulate you?" Sadie asked.

"Are you?" Mariel countered. "Granny, it's not like you to tell others what to do. You've always been so strong, so supportive, but never interfering or demanding."

"I'm not interfering or demanding now," Sadie replied. "I'm just preparing the way for the next generations." She took Mariel's hand in hers. "You can walk away from this at any time, without guilt. I only want you to accept this if it's truly what you want in your heart."

"And you think this is what's in my heart?"

Sadie nodded. "I'm praying that it is, yes. But in the end, I won't force anyone to do anything. I haven't tried to force things with your mother. I never did, even when she married so young to a man I didn't trust—but I'm hopeful."

Hopeful.

Mariel looked out over the lilies. The tall stately plants seemed so silent, so knowing, as if they, too, were listening to Sadie's request. And it was a simple request.

She wanted her family back together.

Why wait until it was too late? Mariel wondered. Why couldn't Evelyn come home now?

A plan formed in Mariel's head. "Granny, what's your one desire?"

"I just told you," Sadie said. "I want to keep this farm intact. I want it to stay in this family."

"And don't you want all of your children to come and visit more?"

"That would be lovely, yes."

"Well, how about we go into action? Easter will be here in a few weeks. Why don't we bring everybody here for Easter dinner? I'll cook or I'll have the food catered, but I think you need this right now."

"Catered?" Sadie stood up, all five feet, four inches of

her. "I have never had an Easter meal catered, and I'm not about to start now."

"Okay, we'll cook together," Mariel replied. "Is it a plan?"

Sadie nodded. "I'd like that."

"Consider it done, then," Mariel told her.

A voice from the edge of the woods caused them both to turn around. "Consider what done?" Heath asked as he emerged from the trees.

Heath saw the startled look on Mariel's face. Her green eyes grew wary. She still didn't trust him.

"I'm sorry," he said as he walked toward them. "I didn't mean to interrupt."

Sadie smiled up at him. "No, no, we were just talking. We've decided to have the entire family home for Easter."

"Really?" He looked at Mariel. She nodded, still silent, still watchful. "Your idea?"

"In a way," she said, her tone defensive. "Granny needs her family around her now."

"But that's a big effort—cooking, preparing."

"I'm going to help her."

Sadie shifted between them. "I'm perfectly capable of preparing a big meal. Been doing it for years."

"But you're—"

"If one more person tells me I'm sick, I'm going to scream," Sadie replied, her voice calm in spite of the threat of a tantrum. "I have heart problems and I'm taking my medicine and trying to adhere to a proper diet. Beyond that, it's in the Lord's hands. But that doesn't mean I have to be shifted off to the old folks' home. Not just yet. And that certainly doesn't mean I can't carry my part of the load. I want my family home for Easter. And that's that."

Heath felt properly put in his place. "I didn't mean to patronize, Sadie. We're just worried about you."

"I didn't mean to criticize," Sadie countered. "And I

appreciate the concern. But if you two want to help me, want to make me feel better, you'll keep doing what you've been doing. Take care of my lilies.''

"We will, Granny," Mariel said.

Heath saw the warning gleam in her eyes. "Yes, we will do that. And I can report that our first shipments went off without a hitch. We've got more trucks coming in next week. Looks like this Easter season is well under way. Might be our best season yet.''

Sadie smiled then. "Well, good. You have brought in some much-needed improvements, that's for sure.'' She started toward the house.

"Wait, Granny," Mariel said, rushing after her. "Let me walk you back.''

"No, you stay and chat with Heath," Sadie said, waving over her shoulder. "I want to be alone for a while.''

Mariel looked puzzled. Shrugging, she glanced at Heath. "Okay, but be careful.''

"I know the way well," Sadie called out. "You two sit and enjoy the sunset.''

Heath didn't think he'd even see the sunset if he sat down with Mariel. She radiated a glow that far outshone the sun. And right now, she looked especially lovely with her fire-tinged hair down and flowing around her shoulders. She wore a short denim skirt and a long-sleeved, lightweight floral sweater.

His heart did that little fluttering thing again.

"Want to sit?" he finally asked, hopeful.

"Sure.'' She sank down on the bench. "So where have you been?''

He indicated the collapsible fishing pole he carried. "I walked down to the pond, hoping to catch a catfish for my supper.''

She laughed, tossed her thick hair, made him swallow

and look away. "So that's what you do with a few hours off?"

"You have a problem with me fishing?"

"Nope. Just figured you'd work right through the weekend."

"Sadie doesn't like the trucks to run on the weekend."

"But you do—*run* that is—I saw you up bright and early this morning, making your rounds through the greenhouses. You're like that little bunny on the battery commercials."

"You got a problem with that, too?"

She shifted, folded her arms over her midsection in a defensive measure. "I don't have a problem with anything you choose to do. I—I just couldn't sleep this morning and I saw you."

"Spying on me, huh?"

"No!" She got up, pivoted to stare down at him. "Why would I have any reason to spy on you?"

He reached out a hand, pulled her back down onto the bench. "Because you don't quite trust me, right?"

Mariel looked at his hand on her arm, but she didn't pull away. "Right now, I don't trust myself. I'm not sure what I'm doing here. I'm confused about this whole setup. And I just figured out from talking to Granny that she's really doing this to bring my mother back home." She stopped, hitched a breath. "She said she wanted to make peace with my mother, even if she'd not be here to witness it. She wants to hold on to this place—"

Heath saw the tears forming in her eyes. His heart hurt for her. "She wants her family to have a safe haven, even if they don't think they need it."

Mariel turned to him then, her green eyes wide. "You do understand, don't you?"

He slowly nodded. Then because he couldn't stop himself, he reached out and pushed her hair off her face. That gesture brought a soft gasp from her parted lips, and brought her head up, her eyes locking with his. "You don't know everything about us though, do you?" she asked. "You don't know about things between my mother and me, between my grandmother and my mother?"

He dropped his hand, shook his head. "Sadie doesn't talk about your mother much. And when she does, she gets this sad look in her eyes. So I don't pry."

"Did she tell you that my parents married very young, when they were teenagers? They had me shortly afterward. That's why I'm so much older than my cousins, even though my mother is the youngest child."

"Should that matter to me?"

She glanced away, but not before he saw the discomfort and shame in her eyes. "It shouldn't matter to anyone, but it does."

Puzzled, Heath didn't know how to respond. "Want to explain that?"

"Not really. You wouldn't understand all the details."

"I'm pretty good at sifting through the details."

"How can you be so sure?"

"Because I'm a good listener. I learn from listening and observing. Just ask the lilies."

She grinned then. "There are a lot of things I need to ask those lilies." Then she gave him a quick glance. "So *you're* the real spy."

"No, yes, maybe. I see things, hear things."

"Did you hear us talking?"

"No. I wouldn't deliberately eavesdrop on a private conversation. I don't have to—I can see the pain of this in your eyes."

She turned away again. She obviously didn't want him to see anything about her.

"Do you want me to leave?"

"No," she said finally. "It's complicated. My mother

hasn't been happy since my father left fifteen years ago. And for some reason, she blames my grandmother...and me, for her troubles.''

He sat back, silent for a minute. Then he decided maybe if he opened up to her, she'd do the same with him.

"I came from a solid family," he said. "My mom and dad were happily married for over thirty years."

Mariel looked up then. "Were?"

"My dad died a few years ago—I think I told you." He shrugged. "When he died, I lost my anchor. We'd always worked together. Without him, I grew restless."

"You told me you traveled?"

"Yes. I was searching for something to replace the emptiness I'd felt since he died."

"And what about your mother?"

"She has a strong faith, and she turned to family. She went on with her life, in spite of the pain."

"I wish my mother could do that."

"She could if she'd—she'd let her family back into her life and turn to God."

He'd expected her to bolt at that suggestion, but instead Mariel's eyes met his again. "Is that what helped you?"

"My faith, you mean? It brought me here," he said, his words low.

She smiled, but looked skeptical. "And so, here we are."

"Yep. Here we are."

"You know, Heath, I think my grandmother has an ulterior motive for bringing me here."

"Oh, and what's that?"

"You," she said softly, simply. "I think she wants us to—"

"Fall in love?" he asked, his breath catching with the suggestion.

She glanced down, embarrassed but amused. "Something like that."

Heath reached for her hair again, his fingers playing through the glistening strands. "That might not be such a bad thing."

She did bolt this time. She stood, moved away. "Or it might turn out to be a disaster."

Then she took off toward the house.

Chapter Seven

Heath stood there thinking he hadn't had any luck tonight with fishing or flirting. Then he threw down his pole and went after Mariel.

He caught up with her on the edge of the yard, near a massive six-foot-tall azalea bush heavy with bright salmon-colored blooms. "Hey, wait just a minute, Mariel."

She kept walking.

He raced to catch her, his arm swinging out to touch her elbow. "Mariel, wait."

She turned finally, her eyes wide, her breath rushing. Then she pushed her hair back and breathed deeply. "I'm sorry."

"No, I'm the one who should be sorry. I didn't mean to scare you off," Heath said, taking a calming breath himself. "I was halfway teasing."

"Oh." She looked down. Even in the waning light of the golden-pink sunset, he could see a becoming flush rising on her face.

Heath kept his smile to himself and his hand on her arm. "I need to know a few things."

"Like what?"

"Well, I've worked with you a week now and I still don't know much about you. You work as a graphic artist, but apparently, you've reached some sort of burnout—"

"I'm tired," she said, her voice low. She sounded fragile…and broken. "Here's the whole story. Years ago, after things with my mother went from bad to worse, I came to live with Granny my last two years of high school—so I do know a few things about this old place. Because I helped out around here after school and on weekends, Granny put me through college at Louisiana State University down in Baton Rouge. I got the job in Dallas straight out of college, and I've been working hard since. I was doing okay until things with Simon got kind of tense."

"Simon?"

"Simon Cassidy, my boyfriend—back in Dallas."

Heath let that soak in. "Your grandmother never mentioned you had a boyfriend."

"She doesn't like Simon. She thinks he's too shallow and self-centered."

"Is he?"

"Well, I didn't think so at first. Granny met him when she came over to Dallas to visit me, and I brought him here a couple of times, but she's never held him in very high esteem. After he made some derogatory remarks about White Hill being 'Hicksville,' I defended him to her. He's always lived in the city, so he can't know about life on a farm. But then I started seeing some of the things she'd already figured out. He *is* shallow and self-centered. So now I'm questioning my judgment."

"What happened? I mean, why did you take a leave of absence and come here?"

She didn't answer him for a minute, but then she

shrugged. "I got overwhelmed at work. I got a raise and big promotion. I guess I thought I'd finally made it. But you know that old saying, 'Be careful what you ask for.'"

Heath nodded. "I know it well. I guess we all experience that at one time or another."

She nodded. "Well, I'm experiencing that now. I've been burning the midnight oil for over a year now, but I've felt restless, the way you said you felt after your father died."

Heath placed his hands in the pockets of his jeans, then rocked back on his brogans. "Sometimes, when we finally have everything we think we want right there in front of us, it's still not enough. In my case, I had a good steady job doing what I enjoyed, then I lost my father. It threw me, made me feel empty and…unsettled."

"That's right." She bobbed her head. "I had something good happen, yet I still felt empty inside. Why is that?"

He took her by the arm again, then guided her up the path to the porch steps. All around them, spring was in bloom. The hot pink azaleas danced in the dusk along the porch railing, holding court over the bright orange and yellow day lilies just beginning to bloom in the rounded beds on each side of the house. Off in the woods, white-petaled dogwood trees sprung out like clusters of popcorn among the oaks and pines.

Heath settled down on a step, then patted the spot beside him. He watched as Mariel reluctantly sank down against the sturdy railing. "I wish I knew the answer to your question. I believe we all start out searching for something, but we wind up finding something else entirely."

She reached out a hand to touch a vibrant red tulip blooming near the bottom step. "It's as if I was constantly spinning, always rushing toward the next goal. I buzzed through college, then worked long, hard hours at my job. I think…after Simon and I had this latest fight, I started wondering what I was trying to prove. Was I doing all of this because it made me happy, or was I just after the recognition, the salary, the image I wanted others to see? Simon said I was being silly, that I'd be crazy to walk away from my job, my lifestyle, in Dallas just to come home on a whim because my grandmother had requested it. And he said I'd be crazy to walk away from him, too. He implied I was lucky to have him.''

This Simon fellow sounded like a real piece of work. Heath was beginning to see why she couldn't trust *him.* "And what did you tell Simon?''

"I told him to give me some time and some space. And I told him I was taking all of my vacation to come home to White Hill, instead of going to Cozumel with him.''

Heath glanced over at her, then leaned close. "You stopped spinning.''

She looked up, her hands tucked around her waist as she leaned forward. "Yes, I stopped spinning. And since I've been here, I've stopped feeling guilty, too. Granny needs me now. I'm glad I came.''

"You said you came *home.* Do you consider White Hill your home?''

Lowering her head, she said, "This place has been more of a home to me than any of the rental houses my mother moved us into. We used to move about every six months, from Louisiana to Alabama and Georgia, then finally Florida. She'd get mad and quit her job, then she'd blame it all on my absent father and the world in general, but mostly she blamed her family and me. Then we'd take off to 'start over.' I got tired of starting over.''

"So you came here to live with your grandmother?''

"Yes. I felt safe here. I found stability here.''

"Maybe that's why you're back now.''

"Maybe.''

She was still looking down. Heath touched a hand to

her shoulder. "Mariel, I don't know what Sadie has in mind, but I'd enjoy getting to know you more. No strings attached."

She laughed, the sound moving over the still earth like a soft melody. "I think that's a given, since we'll be working together until Easter."

He got up then. "Well, it doesn't have to be all work. We could…go to a movie in the city, maybe? Have dinner somewhere. I'd like to see Shreveport. I hear the Red River is pretty, and it does have a rich history."

"It's just a lot of water."

"Ah, but it's all in the eye of the beholder."

She grinned, then reached out a hand. Heath pulled her to her feet, her gesture making him think he'd gained a small measure of her trust after all.

Mariel stared at him, her expression thoughtful, then said, "I guess since you listen to flowers, you probably talk to water, too, right?"

He tilted his head, tossed his long bangs over, then grinned back at her. "No, I mostly drink water. But I talk to trees. Completely different thing. A very one-sided conversation."

"You're strange."

"You're pretty."

She moved away, the wall back up. "Let's make a pact, okay?"

"Okay."

"Let's agree to get to know each other, with the understanding that we're here to help Granny and get these lilies out to our florists and nurseries during the holiday rush. As for all the rest…I don't know. I have a few weeks to decide what to do about Granny's last will and testament—something I refuse to think about now—and I have some time to make up my mind about you."

Heath figured that was the closest thing to a commitment he was going to get from Mariel right now. But he could live with that. "Fine," he said, taking her hand to shake on the pact. "I'm a patient man. I can wait." He met her confused gaze with a calm challenging look. "After all, I said I was only *halfway* teasing about falling for you."

"Well, don't hold your breath."

She said it with a stiff smile and a firm handshake.

Then she turned and went inside the house.

Mariel went straight to her bedroom on the second floor. From the rounded bay window that formed a turret on the top of the house, she had a perfect view of the lily field off to the west. Falling across the cushioned box seat, she watched as Heath walked back down the gravel drive. Watched and held her breath.

He'd been halfway teasing her about falling in love.

Did he feel the things she'd been feeling?

Did his heart move twice as fast each time they were together?

Mariel grabbed a ruffled pillow, clutching it as she studied Heath Whitaker. He was tall and lanky, well muscled from working out in the fields. His California tan and sun-streaked longish hair made him look like movie star material, but his gentle eyes and down-to-earth poetic attitude made him prime falling-in-love material.

Which was exactly what Mariel couldn't do.

She wouldn't fall for Heath, not even if dear Granny wished it. Not even if she herself secretly thought about it. She was too confused, too unsure right now, to even consider that.

Just fantasies, she told herself. Just silly daydreams.

This place had that effect on her. White Hill had always been a whimsical, magical place for Mariel. A safe retreat from her mother's wrath and the world's hard knocks.

Granny Hillsboro was a gentle, loving, undemanding presence in her life, a solid foundation. Mariel had always been able to turn to Granny for unconditional love and nurturing, two things Evelyn had dished out in short supply. Two things her father hadn't cared enough to give her.

Love and nurturing. Two things Heath gave to the land and the lilies each day. The lilies were thriving under his tender care.

Mariel closed her eyes, wondering how it would feel to be in Heath's arms, to let him love and nurture her in the same gentle way he cared about the land and the flowers.

"No," she said, jumping up to toss the pillow back down on the window seat.

"My, my, what did that poor old pillow do to you?" Sadie said from the open door.

"Granny!" Mariel whirled to find her grandmother standing there with a tray. "What's that?"

"Our dinner," Sadie replied, bringing the tray to a round walnut-grained table by the bay window. "Dutch went into town to visit friends. Heath generally spends weekends on his own, working on that old cottage. So I guess it's just you and me, kid. I made us peanut-butter-and-jelly sandwiches and some hot tea. And I have brownies and fruit for dessert."

Mariel sat down on one of the high-backed green velvet chairs next to the small table. "Is this good for your diet?"

Sadie rolled her eyes, then poured tea from a petite silver pot. "The bread is whole wheat, the peanut butter is low-sodium, low-sugar. And the jelly is mostly pure fruit. The brownies are also low-fat. Made them with apple sauce instead of oil or lard. And there's strawberries and bananas on the side."

"You are behaving," Mariel said, relief washing over her as she surveyed the silver tray of food. "Thanks for dinner, Granny. This reminds me of all the tea parties we used to have up here.''

Sadie handed her a floral china cup filled with steaming tea. "It's *green* tea now, darling.'' Then she sat up properly in her own chair like a true lady. "I thought you could use a tea party. You seem to be a tad confused and bewildered by all of this talk about my estate.''

Mariel reached for her grandmother's hand. "I don't like hearing you talk about dying, Granny.''

"Honey, we all have to die someday," Sadie replied. "I don't fear death. I know I'll be going home to Christ.''

Mariel nodded. "You have such an assurance about that.''

"Of course. This life here on earth is just the beginning. I'll be with Jonas again soon.''

Mariel took a bite of her sandwich, still amazed that her grandmother made the absolutely best peanut-butter sandwiches in the world, in spite of the low-fat content of this one. "Why do you suppose Mother never accepted faith the way you do, Granny?''

Sadie placed her cup of tea back on the matching saucer. "I've often wondered and prayed about that. I taught all of my children the same, took them to church each Sunday, tried to model a Christian life for them. But Evelyn was always headstrong and stubborn. As the years went by, she quit going to church, quit pretending to believe. Then of course, she met your father and that was that.''

"And I was the result of *that*," Mariel pointed out. "A mistake.''

Sadie grabbed Mariel's hand back. "Honey, you were never a mistake. You have been a blessing to me.''

"But not to my own parents. I—I think Mother has always resented me. And it's obvious my father never wanted me.''

Sadie sat silent for a minute, then said, "Your mother

loved you—she still does. She just has a hard time expressing that love, after what your father put her through. And truth be told, I never liked the man, but I think *she* drove him away. She could never accept that he truly wanted to marry her. Vincent Evans was a weak man, but he did love your mother. He just couldn't fight her any longer.''

Mariel hung her head. ''And what about me? Did he ever really love me?''

''He loves you,'' Sadie replied, a knowing smile on her face. ''I keep him updated on you.''

Shocked, Mariel stared at her grandmother. ''You've kept in touch with my father?''

''Off and on,'' Sadie said, her hands folded primly in her lap. ''He came back around a few years ago. Didn't want me to tell you, but I think you need to know. Your mother would be furious, of course, if she knew. But since she never bothers to question me on anything or even talk to me for that matter, I decided I'd keep this information to myself.''

''But why haven't you ever told me?''

''I wanted to protect you, darling. I didn't want to get your hopes up, only to let you down. Vincent loves you and knows all about your life, but I don't think he's ready for a reunion. Like I said, he's weak. Maybe one day he'll find the courage to seek you out. I've kept him informed, and beyond that, I haven't interfered. But I've certainly prayed that he would seek you out and make amends for his past actions.''

Mariel understood what her grandmother meant. Sadie had never been one to mind other people's business. Yet Mariel couldn't help but be a bit hurt by this well-kept secret. All those years of wondering and worrying.

''Where is he?''

''He lives in Shreveport. Last I heard, he was working

for one of the hospitals there, as a maintenance man. He never married, but he's had lots of lady friends.''

''That figures.''

Mariel grew quiet, wondering what other secrets her family had hidden deep inside these old walls.

''I'm sorry I never told you,'' Sadie said.

''Why are you telling me now?''

Sadie shrugged. ''Well, you're here for a while. He's near…'' Her voice trailed off. ''I had to wait for the right time.''

Mariel went back to the window. ''I'm not sure this is the right time. I'm so mixed-up, so out of sorts. I don't know why I'm here, I don't know if I want to go back to my job or Simon. I don't think this is the time to have a confrontation with the father who abandoned me.''

Sadie came to stand beside her, both of them gazing down on the white-tufted lilies gleaming in the first light of the moon. ''I didn't suggest a confrontation, dear. I suggested a reunion.''

Mariel turned to face her petite grandmother. ''Is this just one more of those loose ends you're trying to tie up before you…go on to meet your Heavenly Father?''

''You could say that,'' Sadie replied. ''I'd like my house in order when I do move on to eternal salvation.''

''You ask a lot, do you know that?'' Mariel said as she reached out to hug Sadie.

''I only ask what I know you can bear,'' Sadie replied as she hugged Mariel tight. ''And I ask it because I love you. And I know God loves you.''

''I love you, too,'' Mariel said. ''But, Granny, about God—I haven't been as loyal about that as you'd probably like.''

Sadie chuckled. ''Don't tell me that, child. Tell the Father. You know where I stand. Maybe it's time you take a stand of your own regarding that matter.''

Mariel let go of Sadie, then looked down on the lilies again, her heart searching for answers that wouldn't come easily. Then she saw Heath leaning over a particularly tall stalk, his nose touching on the budding tips of a sweet-smelling blossom. The nurturer tending his field.

It was an image she took to bed with her that night.

That same image flowed through her dreams in a sweet song, a song that came singing softly from the beautiful petals of the lilies in the field. In her dream, Mariel could hear the song of the lilies.

But she woke to silence.

Chapter Eight

"Now's your chance," Mariel said to Heath the next afternoon.

He lifted his brows in a questioning look. "My chance for what?"

"I'm going into Shreveport this afternoon, to talk to my uncles about having the family here for Easter. You're welcome to come along."

They'd been to church with Sadie. It was a perfect day for an afternoon excursion. The sun tinged the air with a burnished warmth, the breeze was gentle and nature was exploding in a burst of flowers. Heath couldn't resist the chance to be with the woman in the pretty pink floral dress and matching pink sweater.

The woman who was beginning to show up in his dreams.

"That sounds nice," he said. "But are you sure you want me tagging along when you visit family?"

She nodded, causing her hair to fall over her shoulders and curl around her bare neck. Causing Heath's heart to unfurl like a blossom finding the sun.

"Oh, that won't take long. I just want it clear that I expect all of them to be here for church and dinner on Easter Sunday. It's important to Granny."

Heath sensed it was important to Mariel, too. "Okay, I'll ride along with you, but only if you let me buy you lunch."

Mariel turned to find Sadie and Dutch coming down the church steps. "Granny, do you mind if Heath and I skip your pot roast? We've decided to drive into Shreveport."

Sadie's eyes widened, but she looked pleased as punch. "Of course not, honey. That's just more pot roast for me to send home with Dutch."

Mariel gave Dutch a beseeching look. "Could you give Granny a ride home?"

Dutch bobbed his head, his striped Sunday bow tie turning crooked with the effort. "I'll keep your grandma company, Mariel. Might take her fishing down at the pond."

Sadie huffed, then slapped him playfully on the arm. "I might be up for a nice walk, after my nap, of course."

Mariel kissed her grandmother goodbye, winked at Dutch, then walked with Heath toward her car. "Want to let the top down?" she asked, indicating the late-model convertible.

"That'd be great," Heath replied, grinning. "Nice wheels."

"I got a good deal on it," she explained. "The previous owner treated it with great respect, so it's in mint condition."

"And just waiting for such a perfect day." He helped her with the canvas top, then opened her door.

"Thanks," Mariel said, that becoming blush moving up her face.

Heath came around and got in beside her. "I haven't been in a convertible in a very long time."

Mariel cranked the car, then turned it toward the highway, leaving the tiny church and the dwindling Sunday crowd behind. "When was the last time you were in a car like this?" she asked, her words hitting the soft wind flowing around them.

Heath pushed a hand through his straight hair. "I dated an up-and-coming actress once. She had stars in her eyes and thought she was already a movie star. Spent way too much on her fancy car and wound up having to move back to Ohio."

"She never made it big?"

He shook his head. "Last I heard, she got married and had three kids. Now she writes and acts in plays at the local theater. But at least she's happy."

He watched Mariel's eyes. They were a brilliant green, earthy and lush. She checked the long ribbon of road, then glanced over at him. "And why haven't *you* ever married and had three kids?"

That question shook him. "Oh, you know the old saying. I've never found the right woman."

Mariel tossed her hair out of her eyes, one hand on the steering wheel. "That's a lame excuse."

"It might sound cliché, but it's the truth," Heath said. "My parents had the perfect marriage—loving, close, happy—even when they fought. I guess it's hard to try to expect that standard, but I haven't found it yet, so I'm still single."

"Picky?"

"Let's just say I'm selective." He held his bangs off his face, his arm against the warm red leather of the car seat. Right now, he could narrow that selection down. Mariel Evans was as close to perfect as he'd ever seen, even with her insecurities and doubts. Mariel had a good heart. He knew that. After all, she was Sadie's granddaughter.

Mariel shifted gears, then gave him a long look. "Why are you staring at me?"

Heath decided honesty might work best here. "Because you really are very pretty."

She put her gaze back on the road. "Are you flirting with me, Heath?"

"Can I flirt with you, Mariel?"

"I thought we agreed to a business relationship."

"Hey, you're the one who asked me on this date."

"This is not a...date. You said you wanted to see Shreveport."

"And you're being so very accommodating on that account. Can I help it if I like that dress."

She glanced down at her gathered skirts. "This was my mother's dress. I found it in one of the closets at home."

"A classic," Heath replied. "Like something out of a fifties movie."

Mariel shrugged. "It fit."

"It does fit," he said, tilting his head toward her.

They came to a stop sign and Mariel gave him a warning look. "Okay, enough about my wardrobe, or lack thereof. What do you want for Sunday lunch? Seafood—Cajun or Creole? Soul food? Or a good-old fashioned hamburger?"

Heath frowned in mock-concentration. "Well, that all sounds good."

"Fine, I'll take you to a place that offers all three," she said. Then she shifted gears and blasted off toward the Interstate.

Heath held on, his breath in his throat. Mariel Evans was a woman full of becoming surprises. He sat back to enjoy the ride, and wondered what might come next.

Mariel wondered why she'd gone and asked Heath to come with her to Shreveport. She'd never been one to follow a whim. She'd never been impulsive. Simon had often teased her about being a stick-in-the-mud. He'd told her she needed to lighten up and learn to be more spontaneous.

Well, Simon would sure be proud of her today. Here she sat in a legendary downtown restaurant not far from the Red River, with a man she was only beginning to know and had yet to completely understand. And *she'd* invited him to lunch.

I must have spring fever, Mariel thought as she watched Heath bite into a batch of fried crawfish. He grinned, wiped hot sauce from his mouth, then took a long drink of sweet tea.

While Mariel swallowed back the surge of—what was it?—longing she felt each time she was around him.

"Do I have hot sauce on my nose?" Heath asked her.

"What?" Mariel mentally shook herself. "Oh, no. I was just enjoying watching you eat that. So you like fried crawfish, huh?"

"I do now," he replied. "Strange little creatures, but very tasty."

"We'll have to have a crawfish boil at White Hill," she told him before taking a bite from her shrimp salad. "Dutch can really cook a mean batch of mudbugs."

"Mudbugs?"

"That's what we call them around here. And we also have a hockey team by that name."

"A hockey team in Louisiana? That's different."

"Yes, considering the only ice around here is in the arena. We get snow every now and then, but mostly we just get humidity."

He nodded. "Tell me about it. But the lilies seem to thrive in spite of that. It still amazes me that your grandmother has that wild field growing right up to her yard."

"That's the original garden," Mariel explained. "She'd never change that field. She insists on letting it grow at random."

"Well, that field has been good to her," Heath replied. "I'm very glad to be here helping her keep up the tradition."

"I'm glad you're here, too," Mariel admitted.

He leaned over the small table, causing Mariel to forget the buzz of hurrying waitresses and the noise of happy diners. "Even though you didn't like me at first?"

"Did I say that?" she teased, the intensity of his blue eyes making her question her better judgment.

"Yes, you did," he reminded her. "Hurt my feelings, not to mention my pride."

"I was just looking after my grandmother."

"Sadie is safe with me, I can assure you. She reminds me of my own grandmother."

"Oh, do you keep in touch?"

"She passed away when I was a teenager."

"Oh." Mariel took a drink of water. "I don't want to think about Granny passing away. But she seems to be dwelling on that a lot these days."

"Sadie is a realist," Heath said. "She is a true example of what being a Christian is all about. She's had a good, full life, but she knows there is much more to come."

"And apparently, she's ready to face that."

He nodded, leaned back on his chair. "Does this make you uncomfortable?"

Mariel blinked. "Being here with you?"

He grinned. "Well, that, too. I mean, talking about Christ and death?"

She picked at a slice of Roma tomato with her fork. "No, not really. I haven't been a faithful churchgoer, but Granny always taught me about the Bible and Christ. It's been there inside me, all the time, I think."

"But you seem doubtful."

"I am doubtful. Granny is so firm in her beliefs, but look at her children. Take my parents, for example. They are agnostic to the core. When I was young, I felt torn between my mother's cynical disbelief and Granny's firm encouragements. But I think Granny has won out."

"She is the best example," he repeated, his eyes soft and sincere. "She only wants the best for you, for all her children and grandchildren."

"She told me she's kept in touch with my father," Mariel said, then instantly regretted it. That was not something she wanted to discuss.

"How do you feel about that?"

Mariel shrugged, pushed her salad away. "I don't know how to feel. He left when I was ten and I haven't seen him since. My mother probably did drive him away, just as Granny said. But...I can't understand why he didn't at least try to stay in touch with me." She sat silent, then said, "He lives here, in Shreveport."

Heath lifted a brow. "Do you want to find him?"

"No, not today. Maybe one day."

Heath gave her one of his endearing half smiles. "We could go see him together."

She shook her head. "No, I'm not ready for that. Right now, we need to do our duty and go visit the other wayward relatives. Think you're up to that?"

"I'm up for anything you throw at me," he told her. "The question is—are you up to this?"

She got up, grabbed her purse. "I have to do this, for Granny. But this won't be the toughest part. I still have to call my mother."

Heath held a hand to her arm before they headed out the door. "You're very brave, Mariel."

The intimate husky quality to his voice made Mariel feel as light and mellow as the coconut pie this restaurant was famous for. "I'm a coward, just a determined coward."

They walked to the car, the quaint inner-city neighborhood moving and flowing around them.

Heath turned to her before she could open the car door. "I don't think you're a coward. I admire you for what you're trying to do for Sadie."

His eyes told her he felt more than admiration for her.

And Mariel's heart told her what her head didn't want to accept. She was beginning to admire Heath Whitaker, too. Way too much.

"Let's get this over with," she said in defense of her erratic feelings.

"Okay." He opened her door, then came around to get in beside her. "Then...I want you to show me the river."

Mariel nodded. "If you insist."

"I do." He buckled his seat belt, then leaned close. He stared at her, his eyes moving over her face and mouth, but he seemed hesitant, then backed away. "I think sitting with you on the river is going to be highly romantic."

Mariel swallowed, tried to find her keys. "Oh, do you now?"

He nodded, helped her insert the key into the ignition, his hand over hers while his eyes held hers. "Yep. And I think I'll wait until we get there...to kiss you."

Coming apart like a flower in the wind, she frowned, then pushed his hand away. "What makes you think I'll let you kiss me?"

"I'm just hoping, is all," he replied, his silky bangs falling across one eye. "And preparing the way."

Mariel somehow managed to get the car in reverse. "Preparing the way?"

"I'm giving you warning, Mariel. And time to think about it. I want to get to know you more, and I really want to kiss you. Just keep that in mind, okay?"

"Got it," she said, her eyes on the traffic light, her heart revving right along with the motor of the speedy little car.

She didn't know how she was going to get through a

serious talk with her uncles now. Not when all she could think about was kissing Heath.

And she wondered with a slight trace of disappointment, why did he have to wait?

Mariel had never before been in such a kissing mood. She didn't need any preparation or warning.

And that was what scared her the most.

Chapter Nine

Mariel decided her uncles had run out of excuses. They didn't seem to have a problem getting together with each other and their families on a Sunday afternoon. She had to wonder why they couldn't do the same out at White Hill.

Today they were gathered at Uncle Kirby's sprawling country-club house, the kids enjoying swimming in the kidney-shaped pool, while the brothers and their wives sat around underneath the canopy of a long patio table.

"Mariel, we sure are glad you called, suga'," Uncle Adam said as he ushered Mariel and Heath to two cushioned deck chairs. "And, Heath, always good to see you, too."

Mariel didn't miss the hint of surprise in her relative's expression or words at finding Heath with her. She was still surprised herself, and still wondering about that promised kiss. Putting *that* enticing image out of her mind, she said, "I'm showing off the river cities to Heath. We haven't been over the river to Bossier yet, but I'll make sure he sees that side of town, too."

Uncle Adam chuckled, then handed Heath a glass of lemonade. "Are you a gambling man, Heath?"

Heath sat down, then shook his head. "No, sir. Why do you ask?"

Kirby shot his brother a frown. "We have casinos here now. Brings in the tourists, but my brother is strictly against it."

"And my brother goes to the casinos to stand in line for the buffet," Adam countered. "Or so he says."

"I've been known to drop a buck or two in a slot machine," Kirby replied, shrugging.

"Can we drop this distasteful subject," Kirby's wife, Delores said, a hand on her husband's arm. "I want to hear all about Mariel. How you been doing over in Dallas, sweetie?"

Mariel settled into the overstuffed chair, a tight smile on her face as she gazed at her aunt. She'd always liked Aunt Dee. The woman spoke her mind and kept a tight rein on Uncle Kirby. "I'm doing okay. Just a little restless lately. That why I agreed to come home when Granny called me."

"She snapped her fingers and you came running," Bree, Adam's wife stated with a lift of her perfectly plucked brown eyebrows.

Mariel glanced at her Aunt Breanna—her aunts were known as Dee and Bree, since they were practically inseparable anyway—thinking the older woman hadn't changed her bleached hairstyle or her uppity attitude since she'd left her sorority sisters back at Centenary College. "Granny needed me, Aunt Bree. That's why I'm here."

"Now really," Bree said, leaning forward, her gold rope-chain necklace clinking on the glass-topped table. "Do you honestly want to move back to Louisiana and run that old lily farm?"

"I'm thinking about it, yes," Mariel said, her defenses

rising. No wonder Granny was depending on her. None of this shallow-headed bunch had the brawn to run the farm.

Kirby got up to turn the steaks cooking on the massive gas grill by the pool. "Now, honey, you know how Mama gets. She gets these crazy notions and as she says, that's that. You don't have to listen to her. And we'd certainly understand if you're just humoring her."

"Is that what you think I'm doing?" Mariel asked, her gaze locking with Heath's for a moment. He looked as shocked and uncomfortable as she felt.

"Sometimes we have to humor the elderly," Bree said, throwing a bejeweled hand in the air. "Sadie has good intentions, but…it's time to give that old place up."

"She's not ready to sell out," Heath said, his blue eyes blazing with fire. "And why should she? The lily farm turns a nice profit each year."

Mariel wondered if this visit had been wise after all. It was obvious that Sadie's children cared little about the lily farm or their mother's predicament. But Heath Whitaker did. And for that, she was extremely grateful.

Bree eyed Heath with a keen interest. "I guess you'd be out of a job if that place did shut down, hmm?"

"Aunt Bree," Mariel said, her tone light in spite of her annoyance. "Heath is very dedicated to his work, but he understands this situation. He's done a great deal to improve the overall operation of the farm, but he's not trying to interfere. He was just stating a fact. Granny doesn't want to shut down or sell the lily farm."

"Well, that's fine," Kirby said, "but we don't want to have to deal with the hassle of running the place. We told you, Mariel. We all agree with Mama's plan."

Mariel shook her head. "So you're willing to let me inherit the majority stock of the place, just so you don't have to deal with it. And what about your inheritance?"

"What about it?" Adam asked. "If you decide to keep

the place going, we'll get part of the profits as silent partners.''

"But not *working* partners," Mariel replied.

"We'd rather sell," Aunt Bree said, her eyes a cold blue as she gazed down at her perfect red nails. "Mariel, suga', we simply don't have time to take care of that old place. It's either sell or let someone else do the work."

"While you get part of the profits?"

"If that's the only compromise, yes."

Mariel got up, watching as Heath did the same. Their eyes met and she knew he was probably thinking this family was hopeless. Don't count on them, he was telling her.

But Mariel was too stubborn to listen. "You know, I didn't really come here to hash this out. I came to ask all of you and your children—" she glanced at the pool where the teenagers and several friends splashed and shouted "—to a family get-together on Easter. Out at the farm. You can come for church and stay for Easter dinner."

Everyone started talking at once, each with an excuse as to why that couldn't happen.

"We have our own church here in town," Aunt Bree said, getting up to pour herself another glass of lemonade. "You can't expect us to drag the children out there for the whole day."

"I'm extending the invitation anyway," Mariel said, her gaze touching on her aunt Delores. She'd noticed her aunt had been very quiet during this whole discussion. "What do you think, Aunt Dee?"

Dee stayed still in her chair, but her smile was full of understanding. Running a hand through her clipped gray-tinged curls, she asked, "Well, does Sadie want us to come out on Easter Sunday?"

"Of course she does," Mariel replied. "You all have to understand—she gets lonely. And she's been sick. What could it hurt to have her family around her on Easter? Is that too much to ask?''

Uncle Kirby glanced at his wife. "Dee, I can see those wheels turning in that pretty head of yours. What are you thinking?"

Dee gave her husband a sweet smile, but her hazel eyes held a tinge of steel. "I'm thinking Mariel is right. We should spend Easter with Sadie. We used to have these big get-togethers out at the farm when the children were little, but we've lost that tradition somehow over the last few years."

Bree rolled her over-eye-shadowed eyes. "Now, Dee, you know perfectly well since we've moved into this neighborhood we always have Easter lunch at the club—and we do invite Sadie each and every year. Besides, I've already bought a new dress and everything."

"You can wear it to church out at White Hill," Dee replied in a saccharine tone. "Then you can wear it to regular church and the club the next Sunday...and show it off twice."

Bree gazed over at her, a hand on one hip as she sat back in her chair. "Dee, you take the cake. I'd never thought of it that way. But...still, I'd hate to miss going to church on Easter. I mean, *everybody* comes on that day."

"Yes, the Christmas and Easter crowd does show up," Adam replied tartly, winking at his wife.

Bree made a face, but shut up. Then she lifted her head toward Mariel, her big sunglasses hiding her eyes. "We'll have to discuss this a bit more, Mariel, honey."

Mariel saw the amused expression on Heath's face, but she also saw the disbelief there. He'd probably never encountered anyone quite so flighty as her aunt Bree.

Wanting to leave, she said, "Well, I hope you do think about this. Granny would never command you to show up, of course. She tries so hard to stay out of your lives. But she needs us in her life.'' She smiled at Uncle Kirby. ''I know you help her out a lot, and call her all the time. But sometimes, we…we just need to see each other, to share time together. That's all I'm asking.''

''You've made some valid points,'' Uncle Kirby replied. Then he gave Mariel a quick peck on the cheek. ''We love Mama, honey. But maybe we have been neglecting her lately.''

Grateful, Mariel said, ''This would mean so much to Granny. She loves *all* of her grandchildren.'' She glanced out at the pool. Her cousins had barely given her a wave, let alone taken the time to visit properly. Was that how they treated their grandmother?

''And what about Evelyn?'' Aunt Bree asked, a finger lowering her sunglasses so she could look straight up at Mariel. ''Is she invited to this little reunion?''

''Yes, she is,'' Mariel replied, a quiet need to push her aunt into the pool causing her to grip the back of a lawn chair. ''I'm going to call her tonight.''

''That's sweet,'' Bree replied as she pushed her glasses back up on her nose. ''And good luck with that, too.''

Aunt Delores shot her sister-in-law a disapproving look, then got up to walk Mariel to the gate. ''We'll let you know about Easter, Mariel. But thanks for talking to us.'' She smiled at Heath. ''Are you sure you won't stay for a late lunch?''

''We already ate,'' Mariel replied, relief washing over her. Maybe Aunt Delores and Uncle Kirby would coax the rest of them to come and visit Sadie. ''I hope I didn't make waves, Aunt Dee,'' she said as her aunt looped an arm through hers. Then she laughed. ''No, on second thought, I'm glad I did ruffle a few feathers.''

''You were right to do so,'' Dee replied. ''We haven't been very attentive to Sadie, and I'll admit I'm as guilty as the rest. We get so caught up in our own lives...." She shrugged, then hugged Mariel. "But you did the right thing, since Sadie would never complain herself. I'm going to try and do better by her, I promise." Then she leaned close again. "And I'll push it with the rest of the clan, too."

"Thanks," Mariel said. She waved goodbye as she and Heath walked toward the car.

"That went well," Heath said, his crooked smile for her eyes only.

"Better than I could have imagined," she retorted on a sarcastic note. "I'm sure I won them over with diplomacy and my sweet nature."

"If it helps, you sure won me over," he told her.

It did help, but Mariel wasn't ready to admit that yet.

Chapter Ten

They were sitting beneath a towering live oak, watching the Red River flow by on its way to split between the mighty Mississippi midstate and the Atchafalaya Bay at the Gulf of Mexico.

"This water flows over five states," Mariel said, wondering why she'd decided to give Heath a geography lesson. "It starts in New Mexico and then crosses Texas, Oklahoma, Arkansas and Louisiana." Grinning, she added, "Inquiring minds want to know that."

"Fascinating," Heath replied, his eyes on her instead of the river.

The wind picked up, giving a measure of relief from the sun's warm heat. Somewhere in a cottonwood tree, a mockingbird fussed and preached.

"I could fall asleep right here," Mariel said, acutely aware of his eyes on her, and his earlier promise to kiss her. She was far from sleepy, but she refused to let her racing pulse or Heath's nearness give her the jitters.

Then he inched closer.

"Here, lean on me," he said, the husky tremor of his

words caressing her skin right along with the soft spring breeze. Without waiting for her to reply, he tugged her close until they were both reclining against the ancient tree's massive trunk. Then he wrapped one arm around her and pulled her against his chest. "Comfortable now?"

Mariel thought about pulling away, but it felt so good, so right, being there, that she couldn't move. So she sighed. "Hmm, yes, I guess I am comfortable."

"You guess?"

"I think."

"Don't think," he replied. "Just close your eyes and rest. You just faced the lions and came out pretty much unscathed."

She did shut her eyes, but found it hard to relax with his heart beating so close to her ear, and in the same rhythm as her own. "So you consider my relatives lions?"

"'Lions, and tigers and bears,'" he quoted. She could feel his chuckle all the way down his chest. "Especially Aunt Bree."

Mariel laughed, too. "Bree and Dee—one catty and one caring. It's always been that way. Aunt Dee's kindness balances Aunt Bree's self-centered nature. They're really okay, once you learn how to handle them."

"Well, you did a good job. You stood up to them. It just shows how much you love your grandmother."

"I do love her," Mariel replied as she snuggled into his arms. "Granny took care of me when I needed her, so now it's my turn."

She felt his finger on her chin. Opening her eyes, Mariel also felt the intense heat of his gaze. "What?" she managed to whisper, suddenly becoming *un*comfortable.

"Not many successful career women your age would say that."

"I'm not like other women."

"I'm beginning to see that."

She knew he was going to kiss her, finally. She lifted toward him, her arms going around his neck, as he lowered his head to hers. His lips were soft and sweet, a pleasant contrast to his callused fingers moving across her face. Mariel shifted, her fingers touching on his silky, sun-washed, too-long hair.

In the background, she could hear the sounds of the city. Cars moving on the parkway to the west, horns blaring downtown. Children laughing as they came out of a nearby museum. The sound of a distant train whistle sending out a lonely wail.

And just a faint bubbling, the river below them, moving in a never-ending cycle through swamps and tributaries to the faraway ocean.

Mariel felt as if she were caught up in that current, her limbs becoming washed with a warm sweetness that felt like a cleansing purge.

Heath held her, kissed her mouth, her face, her hair. Then he lifted his head and gave her that endearing half smile. "Now that was worth the wait."

His words brought Mariel up, as if she'd just broken through the waters. "What are we doing?"

"Kissing," he replied, a finger to her mouth.

"No, I mean what are we *really* doing?"

As if sensing her sudden bout of fear, Heath held her away. "We're…following our hearts? Exploring the possibilities? I don't know. Why don't you tell me?"

"I don't know, either," Mariel replied, a warm heat slipping over her flushed body. "I…don't know where this is going." She looked out over the river, then glanced back at him. "What if I don't…agree to Granny's proposal?"

"What if?" He didn't seem too worried about that either way.

Mariel didn't know whether to be sad or glad over the

calm way he'd answered her. "What if I go back to Dallas?"

"I'll come visit you there—always wanted to see the Big D."

That only confused her. "You mean, you intend to follow this to the end, regardless of what decision I make about the farm."

He stared at her for a long time, his unwavering eyes holding his intentions behind a controlled mist. "Yep. I think I just decided that. Must have been the kiss."

His eyes washed over her, making her feel as if she were back in that raging river again. She didn't know if she could survive the depth of these feelings, or the alluring pull of his calmness. "Heath, I just dumped my boyfriend."

"So?"

"So I'm confused, hurt, spinning—"

"I thought you'd stopped spinning."

"I thought so, too. But now, right this very minute, my head is spinning. *You*—you're causing this."

"Let's kiss on it—maybe then your head will feel better."

"No," she said. "I don't think that's wise."

"Let's try it and see."

He leaned close again, then lifted her to him, his arms strong on her back. Mariel didn't resist. She liked his kisses. Liked him. A lot.

But what she didn't like was the uncertainty of it all.

"I'm afraid," she managed to say between kisses.

"Me, too," he said on a whisper just past her ear.

"Really?"

"Uh-huh."

"But you're willing to…try?"

"Yep."

"How can you do that?"

Heath gave up on kissing, for the moment. Then he pulled her close again. "I'm putting my faith in God. In His plan for us."

"You think He has a plan for us?"

"I'm sure of it."

"You and Granny sure make a formidable team."

"We have the Lord on our side."

"I'm not so sure about that. I mean, I'm not as sure as you seem."

He looked down at her then, his finger back on her chin. "Then let me help you—to be sure. I can show you all the small quiet miracles God allows for us, each and every day. I showed you how to handle the lilies, didn't I?"

"Yes, and I appreciate—"

"I want more than appreciation, Mariel."

In his eyes she saw what he wanted.

And even through her haze of fear, Mariel saw that same want inside her own heart. "We still don't know each other very well," she said, trying to be rational.

"I know what's important," he replied, his fingers playing through her hair. "I saw you that day, walking toward the lilies field, and I just…knew. And since then, you've proven yourself in more ways than I ever dreamed. You've worked hard, tackling whatever task I handed out, from potting bulbs to weeding the gardens, to washing up manure. You respect the other workers and…you respect your grandmother. You love White Hill. I can see that clearly enough. And you've come home, Mariel. You've come home to your faith and your center. That's all I need to know." Then he grinned. "And besides, you're so easy to look at, so pretty, so tempting." He said this with a kiss for each compliment.

Mariel swallowed the lump in her throat. No matter how hard she'd worked at creating vivid artwork on Web sites, no one had ever complimented her on her hard work or her inherent need to respect other people. Her bosses had hinted she needed to be more assertive, more ruthless. And Simon had teased her about being so old-fashioned and "countrified," as he used to put it.

The very traits she'd tried so hard to fight off and change for everyone in the big city were the things Heath had just admired about her.

"I'm not so sure I'm all those things," she said, her mother's bitterness and her father's abandonment clouding her mind. "You don't know everything about me, Heath."

"But I'm willing to hear it all," he replied. "We all have bad times, Mariel. We all have things we'd rather keep buried inside."

"You, too?"

"Me, too," he said. "My parents had a perfect marriage, but I never said they had a perfect son."

Mariel couldn't imagine this gentle, poetic man as anything but perfect. And yet, she sensed a steel inside him, a steel forged from hard knocks and tough life lessons.

"Maybe we do have some things in common, after all," she told him.

"We've got some time to find out." He pushed her hair off her face, his eyes touching on her. "There's no rush. No rush at all. It's a new spring, with new flowers everywhere. And those flowers will bloom in God's own time. That always gives us hope."

Mariel became hopeful for the first time in a very long time. She decided maybe she *should* start listening to her heart. And…to those lilies in the field.

By the time they got back to the farm, the sun was setting in pink and gold hues toward the west, out over the stretching green and white of the big field.

Mariel parked the car, her eyes gazing out over the lilies

peeking just over the ridge. "They'll be in full bloom soon," she said to Heath.

He nodded, glanced out into the dusk. "It's a beautiful sight to behold. The walking tours will start next week. And the on-site store will open. I'll need your help."

"I used to work during the tours," Mariel replied, warm memories making her smile as she recalled the hundreds of locals and tourists alike who made the drive out to White Hill each spring to buy lilies or have their pictures taken in their Easter finery in front of the famous naturalized field. "Granny started me out with my own lemonade stand, then advanced me to a salesclerk in the nursery store. Before I left for college, I got pretty good at helping people pick out bulbs and blooming flowers."

"You do know how it works." Heath leaned back on his seat, his eyes on her. "Which is why Sadie trusts you to keep the farm going. Do you realize you are the only one who keeps coming back, Mariel? Her sons keep tabs on her and help her, but they don't actually get their hands dirty, working in the greenhouses and fields. But you, you've actually lived here, worked here—and from what Sadie tells me, you come back each spring to help out and enjoy the blooming season."

"I've tried to be here whenever I could," Mariel replied. "I mean, it's home." She watched as the burning sun glistened like a golden halo just over the horizon. "You want to hear something else about me? Something I don't talk about much?"

"Sure," he said, his finger moving down her arm. "What?"

"I used to paint pictures of the lilies. For a long time, I wanted to be an artist. Granny encouraged this, and urged me to set up my easel and paint the lilies. So the two years I lived here with her during high school, I took art classes and painted. Even won some awards through the art council's ArtBreak—that's a student art festival they put on each spring.''

"That's great," he said. "Do you still paint?"

"No. Not on canvas anyway. I miss painting with a brush.''

"Do you still have some of your paintings here?"

She shrugged. "I sold some of them—to tourists. And I think Granny kept a few. I know a couple of them are hanging in her bedroom.''

"And why don't you talk about this? Don't you do graphic art now in your work?"

"Yes, but that's different. That's computerized—a different kind of challenge.''

She stared out into the sloping field, the scent of the lilies washing over her like a thousand showers of sweet perfume. "I—I think I want to paint again.''

Heath sat up, tilted his head at her. "What's stopping you?"

"Fear," she admitted, almost relieved to have her secret dream out in the open. "I have a degree in Liberal Art, studied art in college. But my practical side won over. I also studied computer graphics and soon realized I could actually eat and pay rent if I went in that direction.''

"You didn't want to be a starving artist?"

"No. I didn't have the courage to test that theory."

"But now?"

"But now, I think I'm ready to try."

"I understand. And I think you should get those paintbrushes out again.''

Mariel looked over at him. He looked sincere, his eyes full of encouragement. "You are so different from Simon.''

"I'll take that as a compliment."

"Simon always teased me about painting. Said I needed

to stick to what I was good at—the thing that paid the bills—the graphic art.''

Heath leaned close, touched a finger to her nose. ''Well, now you don't have to do what Simon says, do you?''

She grinned, leaned her forehead against his. ''No, I don't. I can't begin to tell you how good that feels.''

''I can see it in your smile,'' Heath told her. Then he kissed her. ''Paint your pictures, Mariel. Go for it. You know what you should do? Paint a portrait of Sadie sitting in front of the lily field.''

Mariel opened her mouth, shut it. ''I don't know if I could do that. It's been a while.''

''It'll come back to you,'' he said. ''I think as you sit and paint your grandmother and the lilies, you'll find your answers.''

''And God?'' she asked, hopeful.

''Oh, He's been there all along,'' Heath replied. ''He's just been waiting for you to come back home.''

Hot tears sprang to Mariel's eyes. She wanted to believe Heath's gentle encouragement, wanted to cling to his persuasive testimonies. But how? How did she find the courage to turn it all over to the Lord?

''Just keep listening, Mariel,'' Heath said, as if he'd read her mind. ''Just listen and it will happen. God's love will pour over you and then…you'll understand.''

''I hope you're right.''

They sat silent then, watching as the last rays of the spring sunshine slipped silently behind the trees to the west.

But Heath held her hand the whole time.

Darkness came and a gentle hush fell all around them. And for a brief time, Mariel felt the peace of God's love surrounding her.

Chapter Eleven

The peace Mariel had felt on Sunday was gone by Monday night when she finally reached her mother.

"Mom, it's me, Mariel."

"Well, well. Nice to hear from you. It's been a while."

Ignoring that pointed remark, Mariel said, "I tried to call last night, but you didn't answer." Mariel knew her mother sometimes let the phone ring, especially when she didn't want to be bothered.

"I was out last night."

"Well…how are you?"

"Okay, but…I had to find out from someone at your workplace that you'd taken a sabbatical to Louisiana."

"You called my work?"

"Yes, I certainly did."

Mariel heard the rush of her mother's sigh. Then silence. It was always this way, with her asking hopeful questions, then her mother pausing for dramatic effect.

"Why did you call my work, Mom? Was something wrong?"

"Can't I call without something being wrong?"

Mariel wanted to answer yes, but then usually Evelyn only called with bad news—another breakup with the latest man in her life, another job lost because she couldn't get along with her boss, or another move to find herself.

Pinching her nose to avoid a headache, Mariel said, "Well, I'm glad you called even if I missed the call. And, yes, I did take a few weeks vacation, to visit Granny. She's been sick—heart trouble."

"Heart trouble? How serious is it?"

Hearing genuine concern in her mother's voice, Mariel said, "Pretty scary—her cholesterol was off the charts, and she probably has a blockage of some sort. But the doctors have her on a diet and medication. She needs to go in for more tests, but she's being stubborn about that."

"I'm surprised she's listening to them at all."

"We're making her listen," Mariel said. "I guess we all just seemed to take it for granted she'd live forever."

"We can't take anything for granted, honey."

Thinking that was a different slant, coming from her mother, Mariel decided to be honest. "Mom, the reason I called—I wanted to invite you to come home—for Easter."

Another silence. Then, "What?"

Mariel could just see her mother, a hand pushing at her short, clipped auburn hair, a diet soda by the phone, her vivid brown eyes dark and doubting. "I—Granny and I want to have a family celebration on Easter Sunday. You know, like the kind we used to have when I was little."

"I remember," Evelyn said, the words husky and far-away sounding. "But…I don't know if I can make it."

Mariel pushed at the knot of disappointment in her chest. "Why not?"

"I might be going on a cruise, with Jeff."

"Who's Jeff?"

"A nice man I met at the restaurant where I work now.

He makes a good living selling life insurance and he's... he's good to me. Different from the losers I've been dating.''

"You're working at a restaurant?" Mariel closed her eyes. A few weeks ago her mother had been working in a boutique.

"Yes, a seafood place right on the water. I'm the hostess. And I have to admit, I love it so far."

So far. Mariel wondered how long that would last. "That's good, Mom. But about Easter... You'd only have to take a couple of days. It would mean a lot to Granny."

Another pause. "I'm sure it would. I'll think about it."

That was more than Mariel had expected. "You could maybe bring Jeff with you."

"Yeah, I'm sure he'd get a kick out of seeing that old farm."

Not understanding Evelyn's apparent shame over having been raised on a farm, Mariel said, "The lilies are pretty. They're just about to bloom. The white field smells so good, and the others—the day lilies lining the fence and growing down behind the nurseries—they'll be in full bloom by Easter. Remember, Mom, how you loved the tiger lilies best?"

"I did, I do," Evelyn said, her voice so low, Mariel couldn't miss the catch in the words. "I have some here in my backyard. Did I tell you I bought a little house out near the beach?"

"Really?" Mariel's surprise must have sounded in her voice. She'd never known her mother to invest in anything so permanent. "That's great."

"Jeff helped me with the loan at the bank and everything. And...I've been designing jewelry on the side, to make extra money. Remember the boutique where I used to work?"

"Yes, sure."

"The new manager… You know how much I disliked the lady I worked for before—well, thankfully she's gone, and I get along great with the new boss. Anyway, she's displaying some of my jewelry in the window. It's selling pretty regularly."

Mariel's smile was real. "That is good news. I never knew you liked to design jewelry."

"I never told anyone."

Mariel sank down on a kitchen chair. There was so much she didn't know about her mother. The distance between them couldn't be measured in miles. And yet it was there.

"Honey, I'll see what I can do about Easter."

Mariel knew that was the best she'd get from her mother. Which meant Evelyn would probably come up with a lame excuse at the last minute and not show up.

She hung up, both hopeful and worried at the same time. Something about her mother seemed different. Evelyn had been almost calm, not her usually frantic, bitter self in spite of the veiled comments about Sadie. Maybe the new man in her mother's life was making a difference. Or maybe having a creative outlet had changed her mother's low self-esteem into a more confident attitude.

Restless and too wound up to go up to bed, Mariel decided to take a moonlit stroll along the lane by the lilies. The moon was full, its bright glow spotlighting the sleeping fields and outbuildings in a pale ethereal gray.

It had been a busy, productive day—so busy she'd seen very little of Heath, except to wave to him in passing while she was helping a customer, or to take his gentle orders with a smile and a nod as she supervised one of the trucks being loaded. These next two weeks would be that way—hurried and rushed, filling the local orders, making sure the visitors got the perfect lilies to honor their loved ones. Then come six o'clock the Saturday before Easter, a hush would fall over this farm and woods. Then they would settle in for a quiet preparation, or as Sadie would say, they would celebrate the resurrection of Christ.

This year, Easter took on a new meaning for Mariel. She felt so close to her grandmother and to the Lord.

And she owed this new awareness to Heath Whitaker.

So it didn't surprise her to find herself heading toward the light burning brightly in his little cottage. She wanted to find Heath on this lovely spring night and…see him again, maybe touch him again, or just talk. After all the shallow, mundane things she and Simon had discussed, she truly enjoyed talking to Heath about philosophy and books, and religion, too.

It didn't even surprise her that she had feelings for him. Strong feelings such as she'd never experienced before with any man.

What did surprise her was her acceptance of those feelings, as if they were a natural part of spring, a natural occurrence of some sort of rebirth in her life. Mariel wasn't used to letting things happen naturally. She liked to have a plan, a logical step-by-step reasoning for each move she made.

But Heath had changed all of that.

Maybe that was why she refused to let her conversation with her mother bother her.

Heath gave her new hope, renewed strength and faith in herself. Even if she left the farm and went back to Dallas, she'd always remember him for that at least.

Heath stood at the door of the cottage, watching Mariel walk up the path to his home. He'd always remember her here in the moonlight, her white cotton tunic and frayed jeans making her look like a true flower child as she touched a hand to one of the fat, blossoming lilies, then bent to hold the tender white petals to her nose.

He could almost hear her sigh on the wind.

He could definitely hear the fast-paced beating of his own heart. There was something about Mariel Evans that touched him, made him want to settle down here in this little house and start a family. Something sweet and confusing.

Heath had never been one to settle. Since he'd left California after his father's death, he'd been a wanderer, a nomad searching for a place to lay his head. As he watched Mariel, her dark hair lifting in the night wind, he thought maybe he'd found that place. Maybe he'd found the one woman with whom he could easily spend the rest of his life.

Even if that woman wasn't sure she wanted the same thing.

"Hey, you," he said as he pushed off the door frame and opened the screen door. "Want some ice cream?"

Mariel looked up at him, surprise in her eyes as she stepped up onto the porch. "Ice cream? That sounds good."

He held the door open. "Rocky Road."

"And so fitting," she said as she turned to stare up at him, her eyes as rich and deep as the earth he tilled and plowed.

"Rough day?"

"I had a talk with my mother tonight."

He reached out a hand to her. "Not good?"

She shrugged, followed him into the small kitchen. "Actually, it went better than I had expected, which scares me even more. I'm used to the anger, the harshness. But she seemed different tonight."

"Maybe your mother is becoming mellow."

"Maybe." She smiled, a soft parting of her lovely, kissable lips. "Wouldn't it be something if…I could finally make peace with her?"

"Have you always been at war with your mother?"

"No. But she's been at war with herself for a very long time."

He dished out two bowls of ice cream, then handed her one. "Well, maybe your mother has stopped spinning, too."

Mariel took a big bite, then grinned. "Is this your answer, then? Ice cream?"

"It works. Don't you think?"

"Yes," she said. They ate their ice cream in silence for a while, their eyes touching on each other with each swallow. Then she put her spoon down. "Heath, I—"

"What?"

"Nothing. It's just nice, being here with you. I'll miss this."

"You say that as if you're already planning on leaving. Did you come here to tell me that, Mariel? That you'll be gone after Easter?"

"I don't know why I came here exactly. Except that I was confused and uncertain and I just wanted to see you."

Heath came around the table, pulled her to her feet. "Let's go for a walk."

He guided Mariel out into the lily field, down a path directly in the center of the swaying stalks. All around them, the blossoms looked like linen handkerchiefs dancing in the wind. "Smell that?"

"How can I not?"

"Do you hear the song?"

"Oh, no. Are you trying to get me to listen to the lilies again?"

Heath tugged her close, a hand on her face. "No, I'm trying to get you to listen to your own heart."

Then he kissed her. Her lips, her face, her hair. "I don't want you to leave, Mariel."

She pulled back, her eyes wide. "This…is too fast…too

complex. I'd have to change my whole life, my whole way of thinking. And besides, what can I expect from you? What if you decide to up and leave yourself?''

''I'm not planning on going anywhere.'' Seeing her doubt in the reflection of moonlight in her eyes, Heath backed away, ran a hand through his hair. ''Okay, I won't push you. But promise me something?''

''What?''

''Will you paint that portrait of Sadie, here in the field?''

''Yes. I'd already decided to start tomorrow—if Granny agrees to sit for me.''

He nodded. ''Good. Then I'll have something to remember you by...if you decide you can't stay.''

Chapter Twelve

If you decide you can't stay.

Mariel thought about Heath's words over the next few days. Palm Sunday was coming and then one more week. And she still hadn't decided what to do.

Nothing was going as she'd planned.

She'd planned on having a few weeks' quiet time here with her grandmother, just to sort through her life and maybe make some decisions. That plan had changed the minute she'd seen Heath standing in the field, surrounded by budding, heaven-scented lilies.

She'd planned on setting some priorities, deciding what she wanted to be when she grew up. That had changed when her grandmother had informed Mariel she wanted to leave the farm in Mariel's care, starting now. It was an inheritance of sorts, and a tremendous responsibility. Mariel didn't like being railroaded, and yet Sadie kept insisting she wouldn't force anything on Mariel. Granny was just offering up some options. And yet, sometimes, Mariel felt like one of the lilies being forced to bloom right on schedule.

"Why are you frowning, dear?" Sadie asked from her spot on a wicker chair. "Do I have a June bug stuck to my face?"

Mariel had to smile. She was painting her grandmother. And she couldn't decide if she was doing this for herself or for Heath. "Your face looks lovely, Granny. I'm just concentrating."

"You'll bring on wrinkles."

"Was my expression that bad?"

"You looked as if you'd swallowed a pickle, is all."

Mariel dropped her brush back on the table she'd set up beside her easel. "Maybe we should take a break."

"I'm fine," Sadie pointed out. "It's you I'm worried about. How are things between you and your mother?"

Mariel knew the real question. Was Evelyn coming home for Easter? "I haven't spoken with her since the other night," she said, her gaze sweeping over the canvas in front of her. "But I have to admit, she seemed almost…happy."

"Evelyn, happy?" Sadie smiled, but the sorrow was still in her aged eyes. "I want nothing more before I die, than to see my daughter happy."

Mariel looked down the lane, making sure they were alone. It was late afternoon and the workers and tourists had left. Heath and Dutch had gone into town for some last-minute supplies, and to make a few special deliveries to some of Sadie's oldest customers.

Glad for this time with her grandmother, Mariel sighed, then poured them both some lemonade from a thermos Sadie had brought out to the work area. "Is it me, Granny? Do you think Mother is miserable because of me?"

Sadie sipped her lemonade, then stared up at Mariel. "Now why would you think that?"

"Because…well, you know. They got married because of me."

"They got married because they loved each other."

"But if she hadn't been pregnant—"

"She would have run off with your daddy anyway."

Sadie got up out of the chair, stretched. "Mariel, honey, you can't keep blaming yourself for your mother's short-comings. Take it from one who knows."

"You blame yourself, too, don't you?" Mariel asked, already knowing the answer.

"I did, for years. I guess I still do. Evelyn never knew her father—she was so young when he died. She only had me and her brothers. They ignored her for the most part, and I—I lavished her with love. But it wasn't enough. And it was too much. I smothered her, tried to shape her, force her into something she couldn't be."

Just like a greenhouse lily.

"And she rebelled."

"In so many ways. I had to back away. I regret that we can't be close, but I've prayed that at least she can find a glimmer of the love we once shared."

Mariel tossed her hair back, then lifted her head to enjoy the fragrance of all the flowers blooming in her grandmother's gardens. "Granny, why do you think it's that way with mothers and daughters? Why do we hurt each other?"

Sadie shrugged, pursed her lips. "Maybe so grandmothers can appreciate their granddaughters even more?"

Mariel laughed. "We'd better get back to our task before the sun goes down and I can't see enough to paint."

Sadie settled down in the high-backed wicker chair, then smoothed the gathered skirt of her floral dress. "Make me look younger, all right?"

"I'm trying to paint you the way I see you," Mariel said, her brush stroking across the rough canvas. "It sure feels good to have a brush in my hand again."

"Don't know why you ever gave it up," Sadie retorted.

"Me, either." Mariel gave the portrait a critical appraisal. "I'm a little rusty."

"I'm sure it will be nice."

"Granny, I don't know if I can do this."

"Of course you can. I can't be that hard to capture."

"No, I don't mean the painting. I mean, giving up my life in Dallas to move back here. I understand…how you want things…if—"

"If I go to meet my Maker."

Mariel nodded, refusing to even consider that. "But I just don't get why you want me to start now."

Sadie gave her a soft smile. Mariel immediately tried to capture that very smile with her brush. Now if she could just read the thoughts behind the smile. "Granny?"

"Oh, all right. I think you and Heath make a good match."

Mariel shook her head. "Now, why does that not surprise me? I figured that out from day one. But why are you pushing for me to come back here now?"

Sadie stopped smiling. "I'm being selfish, darling. I get lonely out here. Dutch tries to keep me company, tries to court me, if you get my drift. But…I miss having children around. I miss my family. I just decided I could count on you."

"You know I'll take care of you, don't you, Granny?"

"Yes, but I don't want to force anything on you—that didn't work with your mother. Let's just keep praying on it." Then she winked. "And besides, if you're not here, Heath can't court *you*, now can he?"

"Somebody mention courting?"

They looked up to find Dutch and Heath coming up the path.

"We didn't hear the truck returning," Sadie said, a becoming blush cresting on her powdered cheeks.

"We parked down by the back nursery," Heath explained.

Mariel lifted her brows. "Didn't hear you walking up, either."

"Too intent on that fancy painting, I 'magine," Dutch said, his eyes twinkling as he stepped close to survey the work-in-progress. "And it shore is pretty, Sadie Girl."

"Oh, pooh." Sadie waved a hand at him, but blushed all over again. "You two get your business taken care of?"

"Yes, ma'am," Heath replied, his eyes on Mariel. Then in a low voice, he added, "You look so natural, doing that."

"She's a born artist," Sadie proudly announced.

"I think you're right." Heath held Mariel's gaze, his eyes as velvety blue as the irises growing down by the duck pond. "It's coming along."

Mariel didn't miss the hidden meaning in his words. Did he mean the portrait of her grandmother, or the growing relationship between the two of them?

Mariel didn't get an answer to that question. They heard a car roaring up the drive right in front of the house.

A petite woman wearing a broomskirt skirt, denim jacket and dark sunglasses stepped out of the car.

Mariel squinted against the growing darkness, trying to see who had come for an evening visit. Then the woman removed her sunglasses and turned to face them.

"Evelyn," Sadie said, a hand coming to her throat.

Mariel searched her grandmother's stunned face, then turned back to the woman. "She's right," she said under her breath to Heath. "It's my mother."

They were sitting in the living room, drinking decaf. Mariel had served the low-fat apple pie she'd baked earlier. And now they were stuck in an uncomfortable silence. She, her mother and her grandmother.

Dutch and Heath had disappeared shortly after the awkward introductions and hellos.

"Mom, I'm glad you came," Mariel said, her gaze sweeping over her mother's oval face. "It's just such a surprise."

"Can't I surprise you now and then?" her mother asked, one finger playing with a looped gold earring hanging beneath the fringe of her dark red hair. "You did invite me, remember?"

"I know, I know," Mariel said, nodding. "But you're early."

"I can leave if I've caused a problem." Evelyn glanced at Sadie. "Mama, do you want me to leave?"

"Of course not," Sadie said.

She'd been unusually quiet tonight. And she looked pale. Mariel's heart ached for her grandmother.

Evelyn crossed her legs, then let one booted foot swing. "I came early because…well…Jeff pulled a stunt that scared me. I needed to get away and think."

Mariel's stomach churned. "Did you break up with him?"

Evelyn shook her head. "No, nothing like that." Then Mariel watched in amazement as tears gathered in her mother's brown eyes. "The silly man asked me to marry him."

"Mother, that's wonderful," Mariel said, releasing a breath. "So what was your answer?"

"I told him I needed to think about it," Evelyn replied, sniffing. "I just don't know."

"What's to know?" Sadie said at last. "If he's a good, decent man, what's holding you back?"

"Is that all that's important to you?" Evelyn countered. "That he's good and decent?"

"It counts in my book, yes," Sadie replied, her green eyes sparking with a fire of defiance.

Mariel was beginning to see that this feud went two ways. She'd never seen her grandmother act rude to anyone, so it shocked her to watch Sadie clam up and purse her lips as she stole glances at her wayward daughter.

"You deserve someone nice and decent, Mom. I think that's what Granny's trying to say." She shot Sadie a warning look, and got a stern frown in return.

"Well, let me assure you he is both," Evelyn said, getting up to pace around the room. "Jeffrey Matthews is... He's different. He encouraged me to start back designing my jewelry, even helped me get up the courage to display some of it in the boutique." She wrapped her arms against her midsection, stared out into the night. "He even talked me into apologizing to that mean old woman I used to work with at the boutique. And he helped me get a good job at the restaurant."

"Sounds like a miracle worker to me," Sadie said, her own arms placed across her chest in a defensive stance.

Evelyn whirled to glare at her mother. "He is good to me, Mama, believe it or not. He says he loves me just the way I am."

Mariel got up to come and stand beside her mother. "Then why did you...run from him?"

Evelyn glanced up then, her eyes as deep and rich as the earth out in the fields. "What if I mess this up, Mariel? Everyone knows I always mess things up."

Mariel saw the fear and honesty in her mother's eyes. "You won't mess up, Mom. Give it a chance."

Sadie got up, too. Slowly she made her way to the window. She didn't reach out to Evelyn. She just stood there. Then finally she spoke. "You came to the right place, Evelyn. If you're searching for answers, you came to the right place."

"Did I?" Evelyn asked, her gaze moving from her daughter to her mother. "Do you even want me here?"

"Of course we do. Don't we, Granny?"

Sadie nodded. "Evelyn, you are welcome here anytime. This is your home."

Evelyn shrugged, her eyes straight ahead. "Well, then I'm home for Easter—early. I hope everybody can live with that."

"I think we can," Mariel replied. "I know we can."

Sadie turned then, her eyes landing on the necklace Evelyn was wearing. "Did you design that?"

Evelyn touched the chunky beaded necklace and smiled. "Yes, I did. What do you think?"

"Interesting," Sadie replied. "Why don't we have some more decaf and you can tell us all about it?"

"All right." Evelyn followed her mother back to the chairs.

And Mariel glanced out into the lily field and said a prayer of thanks and hope.

Chapter Thirteen

"Well, the house is still standing," Dutch said under his breath to Heath early the next morning as they headed toward the nursery. "That's a good sign."

Heath glanced up at the imposing white house, his gaze automatically going to the tower room—the room that had always been Mariel's, according to Sadie. "Do you think Evelyn will cause trouble?"

"Evelyn is trouble," Dutch said, shaking his head. "Bless her heart, she's just got a chip on her shoulder and nobody can knock it off. Nearly broke Sadie's heart when she took Mariel away from here all them years ago."

Craving more information, Heath stopped on the path. "Why did Evelyn move away?"

"Wanted to distance herself from the pain—the divorce was hard on her and the child." He took his faded cap off to scratch his head. "Vincent Evans was a charmer. But he never grew up. Thought he could charm his way through life. Evelyn loved him—too much. She never got over him."

"And Mariel? She never talks about her father. Were they close?"

"Mariel loved him, too. But Vincent just considered Mariel like a baby doll—something to play with then tuck away. Vincent never had sticking power."

Heath watched as Dutch ambled toward the first greenhouse, where the trucks were already lined up to move out another shipment of lilies—a rare weekend shipment since they'd had extra orders this week.

"Sticking power," he said to himself. Mariel had questioned him about his own sticking power. That certainly explained a few things.

Maybe she thought all men were just like her father.

Heath thought he'd just have to prove her wrong. But his time was running out. Tomorrow was Palm Sunday. One more week until Easter. How could he prove himself in a week?

Heath stared out into the distant lily field. Budding flowers sprouted like teardrops from the tall swaying stalks.

Flowers.

Heath smiled. He decided it was about time he started wooing Mariel. He would romance her into accepting him.

And somehow, he would convince her that together they could both be happy here at White Hill.

It was a good place to put down roots.

"So, that's everybody," Sadie said, turning from the phone to smile at Mariel and Evelyn. "The whole gang is coming out tonight for a cookout and crawfish boil."

"And Dutch will be cooking the crawfish?" Evelyn asked from her spot at the kitchen table. She sat wearing a frilly white cotton blouse and jeans, sipping her coffee as she skimmed the *Shreveport Times*. But Mariel noticed her mother's eyes looked red-rimmed, as if she hadn't slept very well.

"You better believe it," Sadie said, bringing the coffeepot to Evelyn for a refill. "That old coot won't let anybody else near the crawfish pot. I'll go down and talk to him and Heath—send them into town later to get supplies." Then she added, "And I could use you two in the gift shop. It'll be packed today."

"I'll be there, Granny." Mariel leaned over the sink, staring out the window. She'd seen Dutch and Heath headed toward the nurseries and greenhouses. They had one large order to fill this morning and then they'd give a few tours this afternoon when the crowds started pouring in. It was that time of year, a holiday season. Even though all the Easter lilies weren't in full bloom yet, most of the other foliage was bursting with color. Happy families would parade around the lily farm, taking pictures in front of the azaleas and daylilies, the Japanese magnolias and the dogwood trees.

Mariel stood there thinking this wasn't such a bad way of life. Especially if she could see Heath coming up that path every morning.

"Where are you, girl?" Evelyn asked from beside her.

"Oh, just thinking," Mariel said, smiling over at her mother. It was odd, having Evelyn here. Odd, but comforting. So far, things were calm and peaceful between her mother and grandmother. So far.

"About that tall, good-looking man out there with Dutch?"

Mariel jumped as if her mother had tickled her. "Oh, him?"

"Yes, him." Evelyn gave her a knowing look. "Sadie and I had a long talk last night after you went up to bed."

"Did you now?"

"Uh-huh. Heath Whitaker, is it? Just about your age, maybe a little older. Handsome, hardworking. My mother is up to her usual tricks."

"I heard that," Sadie said from behind them. "Doesn't hurt to introduce Mariel to a fine young man."

"What if Mariel isn't interested?" Evelyn asked, a touch of the old rebellion in her words, her eyes on Mariel. "Of course, I think I see some interest in her eyes. She can't seem to peel them away from Dutch and Heath. And I don't think she's looking at Dutch."

Sadie actually laughed.

Mariel gave her mirth-filled grandmother a sharp look, then turned to her mother. "Heath and I are just friends. He's showing me the ropes—everything there is to know about growing lilies."

"Why on earth do you need to know how to grow lilies?" Evelyn asked as she pushed a hand through her short, clipped hair.

Mariel looked at Sadie. Her grandmother sent her a raised-eyebrow warning. "We didn't discuss that part last night."

"What part?" Evelyn asked, frowning. "Is there something I need to know?"

Mariel could see the nice, peaceful morning about to evaporate right along with the dew. "Granny wants me to consider taking over the farm."

Evelyn slumped back against the counter. "What?"

Sadie drummed her fingers on the table. "I've asked Mariel to come home to run the farm. The boys want to sell it and put me in a fancy retirement home closer to them. I don't want to sell and they don't want the responsibility of running the farm. So I asked Mariel."

Evelyn's round dark eyes flashed as she blinked. "Mariel, how do you feel about this?"

"I'm still debating," Mariel said, trying to be honest with her mother. "I'll be here through Easter."

"And after that?"

"I don't know yet, Mom. I was getting restless with my

job in Dallas. And Simon and I broke up. It seemed like a good time for a change.''

"And you call coming back to this place a change? I mean, a change for the better?''

"It could be,'' Mariel said, trying not to sound defensive. "Besides, this is all speculation. I haven't decided what I'm going to do. But I don't want Granny to lose this farm.''

The silence in the room seemed to echo through the house like a ticking clock. Mariel waited for the outburst, for the accusations, for the harsh words she knew her mother must be thinking. But Evelyn surprised her by just standing there, her arms wrapped against her chest, her gaze downcast.

Then Evelyn turned to Sadie. "I don't want to sell this place, either.''

"You don't?'' Sadie asked, her hand going to her throat.

"Of course not.'' Evelyn shrugged. "I mean, I know I haven't exactly been in on the day-to-day operations, and I've never asked you for one dime of the profits, but…this place is home.''

"It is home,'' Sadie said. "And I won't sell it unless it's a last resort.'' Then she looked up at her daughter. "But, Evelyn, I would have thought you'd be the first to want to get rid of it.''

"You thought wrong,'' Evelyn said, her eyes bright with tears. "And I can't blame you. I haven't been back to visit very often and I certainly haven't offered you support.''

"No, you haven't. But you're here now,'' Sadie said as she got up to come and stand in front of her daughter. "And I'm grateful for that.''

Mariel watched in amazement as the two women she loved most in the world stood just a foot apart, staring at each other. She knew her grandmother wanted to hug Evelyn close, but Sadie refrained from that. And Evelyn held her body tightly against the counter.

"But, Mother," Evelyn finally said, "is it right to place such a responsibility on Mariel?"

"I'm splitting the farm stock and holdings four ways, with Mariel getting the majority if she decides to take over," Sadie said. Then she calmly explained her plan. "I hope you are agreeable to this."

Evelyn's eye grew wide. "You're talking about a will."

"Why, yes. I'm getting old, in case you haven't noticed."

Evelyn's expression changed as her eyes grew wild and dark. Then she turned to Mariel. "She's not just sick. She's talking as if she's going to die."

"I know," Mariel said. "You get used to it."

"Don't make fun," Evelyn said, the words a whisper. Then she burst into tears and ran out the back door.

Sadie lifted her brows in confusion, then turned back to Mariel. "That went better than I had expected."

Mariel found her mother down by the pond, where the water lilies and daylilies rivaled each other for attention underneath the clumps of moss-draped bald cypress trees. This had always been her mother's favorite spot.

Evelyn was sitting on a bench, one of many placed around the property for family and tourists alike to enjoy at random.

"Are you all right?" Mariel asked as she sat down beside her mother on the long willow-bark bench.

"I'm fine. Hormones, I suppose."

"Hormones?"

"I'm getting older myself, Mariel."

"Yes, I guess we all are."

Evelyn sniffed, wiped her eyes. "It's just that it all hit me—how I've been so selfish. Jeffrey's tried to tell me I needed to mend some fences. I guess I finally saw what he's been talking about. I mean, I've never actually thought about how I'd feel if my mother died. Especially if we left things so…unsettled between us.''

Mariel didn't say anything. She knew her mother didn't need platitudes right now. After a while, she asked, ''Jeffrey? Jeff—he's helped you?''

Evelyn looked around at her. ''Jeff is a Christian. He goes to church every Sunday, serves on church committees. It scared me at first—I thought he'd act like Mama and push me to follow the straight and narrow. But Jeff's…different. He's gentle and understanding, and he's so kind. But he's also handsome and distinguished. He just has everything together.''

Mariel understood now. Jeffrey sounded a lot like Heath. ''And that scares you?''

''Very much. Scared me into running back here.''

''Yes, I guess you'd have to be pretty scared to make this trip.''

Evelyn smiled at that. ''I've wanted to come home, but I was always afraid Mama and I'd just get into another fight.''

''She loves you.''

''I know that. And I love her. I just feel as if…I've disappointed her so much.''

''Because of me?''

Evelyn lifted a hand to her mouth, her eyes going wide. ''Oh, baby, is that what you think?''

''You did have to get married because of me.''

Evelyn shook her head. ''I got married because I loved your father so much, I would have done anything to be with him.'' It was a bitter statement reminiscent of so many of the conversations they'd had over the years.

Mariel didn't respond to that. She still had to wonder if her mother regretted having her so young. But she wasn't going to push that issue. "I'm glad you came home, Mom."

Evelyn took Mariel's hand. "Me, too." She looked out over the little pond, her gaze following a mother duck and her four baby ducklings as they trailed across the water on the other side. "I have to decide…about marrying Jeff."

"Seems we've all got some decisions to make."

Evelyn glanced away from the ducks, then shifted her head around to stare behind Mariel. "Seems that way. Your lily man is coming."

"My lily man?" Mariel lifted her chin.

"Heath Whitaker," Evelyn whispered. "He's walking toward us. And from where I'm sitting, it appears he only has eyes for you."

Chapter Fourteen

Heath looked down at the two women perched on the aged bench like pretty birds, chatting in the morning sun. "Morning, ladies."

"Hi." Mariel's expression bordered between bemused and aggravated. Maybe he should just leave them alone. But Sadie had insisted he come and find them, check on them.

"Am I interrupting?" he asked for manner's sake, his gaze still intent on Mariel. "Sadie was worried."

"No need to worry, and no, you aren't interrupting," Evelyn said, rising from the bench with a sidelong glance at her daughter. "I'm going back to help Mother open the gift shop. I'll see you in a bit, Mariel."

"Okay." Mariel watched her mother leave, her eyes pensive and full of wonder.

Heath sat down next to her. "Sadie sent me. Honestly."

"I believe you. Honestly. She was probably afraid we'd get into a brawl."

"Didn't look like you two were fighting."

She brought her head around, her eyes watchful, cautious. "No, we weren't. My mother has changed, I think. She seems softer around the edges, more gentle and calm. I think she's in love."

He smiled at that. "Love can do that to a person."

She looked away, out at the pond. "We need to get back. We've got a busy day."

Heath wished he could make her trust him. But then, he was beginning to understand all the many reasons why she didn't trust anyone. "Yep. And I hear we're having a big to-do tonight."

She nodded. "The whole family. Granny is thrilled, of course. First Easter, and now a Saturday-night get-together."

"And what about you?"

"I'm handling everything in bits and pieces, just waiting for the next surprise."

Or the next disappointment, Heath reasoned.

"How about we get away for a little while? Say tomorrow night?"

"You're asking me on a date?"

"I think I am."

"No surprises?"

He grinned. "Well, maybe a couple."

She got up, picked up a rock to skip across the still water. "You know, Heath, I like things civilized and orderly. Simon used to call me a stick-in-the-mud. But that's just the way I am."

Heath came to stand beside her, to still her upraised hand. "If you're trying to warn me, or scare me away, or if you're trying to tell me you can't change for me, well, that's okay. I don't want you to change."

She dropped the rock she had been about to throw. "You *do* continue to surprise me. It seems my whole life everyone's wanted me to change—except Granny. She is so accepting of people."

"So am I."

"That's probably why she wanted you and me to—"

"Fall in love?"

"Are we—falling in love?"

He pulled her close, then pushed at the ruffle of hair moving across her face. "We might be. It's happening fast at times, but other times, it can't happen fast enough."

Mariel looked up at him, her eyes full of questions and secrets. "I don't understand—"

He cut off her doubts with a kiss. He didn't hurry it or confuse the issue. He just enjoyed the touch of her lips to his, warm and inviting and soft as a sigh. Then he lifted his head and stared down at her. "Sometimes we don't need to understand. We just need to let nature take its course."

"Like growing lilies?"

He nodded.

"But sometimes we have to force the lilies to bloom."

"Yes, and then, sometimes we just sit back and watch them bloom, like in Sadie's field. There's something simple and beautiful in just letting nature take its course."

"That takes patience."

Heath put his arm around her as they started back toward the house. "I'm a very patient man."

But he was fast losing his patience, Heath thought later that night.

The family was gathered around several picnic tables in the sloping backyard. The night was warm with a springtime tinge of a breeze, the perfumed scents of all the flowers lifting up to merge with the spicy smell of cooked crawfish and freshly baked apple pie.

Heath had been following the undercurrents of this family reunion. The two brothers were jovial enough, but clammed up whenever their sister, Evelyn, approached. Sadie tried to keep everyone laughing as she joked with Dutch, but Heath could tell this happy occasion was taking its toll on her.

At least the other grandchildren were enjoying helping Dutch cook the mudbugs, when the boys weren't chasing the girls with the still-alive critters just before the crawfish met their fate in the boiling pot.

Aunt Delores was pleasant and helpful, while Aunt Bree seemed to be pouting and begging for attention. Heath had noticed Bree's hostile looks and saccharine smiles each time she and Evelyn crossed paths. Bree seemed to resent Mariel's mother.

Heath sat apart from the rest, his eyes following Mariel. She'd been a bit standoffish since he'd kissed her this morning. She was being civilized, but he could tell in the way she tried to avoid any eye contact with him, that she was very much aware of him.

As was her observant mother.

Evelyn came over to him, handing him a piece of pie. "You shouldn't eat alone."

"I'm just allowing Sadie some time with her family."

"According to my mother, you're like a member of the family."

"Do you mind that?"

Her eyes held a trace of daring. "I don't mind at all. I really have no say in the matter. But I don't want to see my daughter hurt."

Heath thought that an odd statement, considering Evelyn had been absent for most of Mariel's life—at least emotionally anyway. "I don't intend to hurt Mariel. I think she's been through enough from what I've heard."

Evelyn raised a dark winged eyebrow. "And what's that supposed to mean?"

Heath didn't want to cause a scene with Mariel's mother, so he said, "It means that whatever happens between Mariel and I should stay that way—between the two of us."

Evelyn nodded, but the look she gave him reminded him of the mother duckling protecting her babies down on the pond. It brooked no arguments. "I guess I deserved that. I don't have the right to interfere, but…there's a lot of water under the bridge."

"So I see," Heath replied, indicating his head toward the group. Then he added, "Mariel is strong. Give her some credit."

"Maybe you're right."

Evelyn sauntered away, not quite smiling, only to be replaced by Aunt Bree, her smile as fake as her eyelashes. "Hello, Heath. Want some coffee with that pie?"

"No, thanks." He studied Mariel's aunt with an amused eye. Dressed in bright pink capri pants and a white short-sleeved sweater, Bree Hillsboro looked like any high-society woman. But there was something about her Heath didn't trust. He immediately had his radar on.

Her jewels flashed as she waved her hand in the air.

"I don't get you," Bree said with unabashed frankness. "Why are you sitting over here staring holes through Mariel when everyone knows you have a thing for her?"

That brought Evelyn, who'd been listening from a few feet away, back. With that same matronly, overprotective look. "Bree, why don't you mind your own business?"

Bree whirled, a glass of soda sloshing in her hand. "Excuse me?"

"You heard me," Evelyn said, her dark eyes smoldering. "All evening long, you've been teasing Mariel about Heath, implying certain things about their relationship. And now, you've come to harass Heath, too? You never were very subtle."

Bree pushed at her teased blond hair. "Honestly, I have no idea what you're talking about. And you are certainly a fine one to talk, considering how you've never lifted a finger to help this family."

"Me? Me?" Evelyn advanced, a finger jabbing at her chest with each word. "You have no idea about me, Bree. You're too wrapped up in your own life to care about anyone else."

"Well, that's a fine thing to say," Bree replied, her voice becoming shrill. "At least I've been here, helping Granny out, while you…what exactly have you been doing the past ten years, Evelyn?"

Sadie came hurrying to them. "Okay, ladies, that's enough. Bree, we're very glad to have Evelyn home again. No questions asked."

"Oh, really?" Bree blinked, a hand on her skinny hip. "And just why is it, pray tell, that she suddenly shows back up right after you've announced the proposed contents of your will? Did anyone else stop to think about that, or is it just me?"

Mariel stepped forward. "It's just you, Aunt Bree. Mother is here because I invited her. She didn't even know about the will until Granny told her."

Bree shot a doubtful look toward Evelyn. "You expect me to believe that?"

Evelyn looked down at the ground. Heath could tell she was struggling for control. "I've never taken any money from Mother before. Why would I be worried about it now?"

"Why, indeed?" Bree spun around like a top, waving her hands. "Look at this place. You could have a nice retirement here, with your daughter in charge. Seems mighty convenient to me."

"Bree, why don't you go get some more ice, and try to cool down?" Adam said, taking his wife by the arm. "We don't want to upset Mama."

But Bree wasn't ready to give up center stage. "Of

course we don't want to do that. I just want some answers. After all, this involves my children and their future, too."

Heath noticed her children and their cousins had become quiet. The four teenagers looked embarrassed, but rolled their eyes with a typical show of disinterest when Aunt Delores tried to comfort them.

"Your children will have a part of this place," Sadie said. "I've made sure no one gets left out."

"That was considerate," Bree replied sweetly. "Except you're making very sure Mariel gets just a bit more than the rest. That kinda stings."

"Does it now?" Sadie replied, her eyes sparking fire. "Since Mariel is the oldest, and since Mariel is the only grandchild who's ever showed an interest in this place, I think I've been fair. I love all of my grandchildren, but I had to make a decision. This is what I've decided. No one will go hungry around here, and no one will be left out, regardless."

Bree chuckled. "You mean, regardless of how we've neglected you?"

Evelyn touched on Bree's arm. "That's enough. We've all neglected Mother. And yet, she continues to forgive us. That's why I'm here, Bree. I've met a man who made me see that I needed to…make a few changes in my attitude."

Bree pushed at her. "And just in time, too, I might add."

"You're hopeless," Evelyn said, whirling to stomp away.

"Not as hopeless as you," Bree shouted.

The silence that followed that shout seemed to ring through the trees and echo out over the fields and woods.

Heath saw the pain on Mariel's face as she looked from her grandmother to her mother. Then she glanced over her shoulder at her aunt Bree. "I'm sorry about that, Granny."

"No need to apologize," Sadie replied softly. "Bree's

had a burr in her bonnet for a long time. Now I think I understand why.''

Heath watched as Sadie seemed to go pale. She turned, reaching for Mariel's arm.

Alarm coloring her face, Mariel caught her grandmother. ''Granny?''

Heath saw the fear on Mariel's face, then looked at Sadie. She didn't look well. She stumbled against Mariel.

''Help me,'' Mariel said. ''Help me get her to a chair.''

Heath rushed forward, along with the brothers and Dutch, who'd been watching the whole scene.

''Better get her to town,'' Dutch shouted. ''To the hospital. And don't wait for an ambulance to come way out here.''

''Granny?'' Mariel asked, as she and Heath held Sadie. ''Do you want one of those pills the doctor gave you?''

Sadie shook her head. ''Too late,'' she said on a weak whisper. ''I think…I'm having a heart attack.''

Chapter Fifteen

"Well, at least Granny got her wish," Mariel told Heath the next night as they sat in the hospital waiting room.

Heath held his head down as he stared into the ice left from his soda. "What's that?"

"All of the family is here." Mariel knew she sounded bitter. "They had to get into a nasty argument, right there in front of her. I don't know what provoked Aunt Bree—"

"Jealousy," Heath replied, the one word a whisper.

Mariel glanced down the hall where her relatives were gathered in a tight cluster. They'd been taking turns at visiting with Sadie the few minutes they were allowed. "But what could she possibly be jealous of? She has everything!"

"Except Sadie's respect," Heath said. He reached a hand toward Mariel, and grateful, she took it.

"I'm so tired," she told him. "Tired of trying to keep them together, tired of trying to make them see. Aunt Bree has always had a spiteful streak. I just never knew how much she resents my mother, until last night.''

''Well, at least Evelyn held her ground.''

''And her dignity,'' Mariel replied. ''I can't believe how well she's handled…everything. She even accepted Aunt Bree's apology with good grace. Maybe she has changed. Maybe this will change all of them.''

''They do seem a bit more somber,'' Heath said. ''This has scared them.''

Mariel gave him a halfhearted smile. ''It sure shut up Aunt Bree. She's being very sweet.''

''We all tend to get mellow with age, and your aunt Bree looks as if she's aged overnight—and matured.''

Mariel had to laugh at that. Heath was in the prime of his life, handsome and healthy. He looked as if he'd been born mellow and mature. ''Thank you,'' she said, tears misting in her eyes.

''For what?''

''For being here. For holding my hand.''

''Even if you don't want your hand held?''

''You noticed that?''

''I've noticed a lot of things about you.''

''And yet, you've stayed.''

''Does that surprise you?''

''I didn't… I wasn't sure you would.''

He didn't seem shocked by her admission. ''I figured that out the day we met.'' Then he added, ''Okay, Dutch explained a few things to me, too.''

''Poor Dutch.'' Mariel shook her head. Dutch sat alone in a chair, his scruffy face in a perpetual state of worry. ''He loves my grandmother so much, but he shouldn't go around telling our family secrets.''

''No secret—it's pretty obvious. You have some issues with…trust, right?''

''You could say that.'' Then she turned to face Heath.

"I just always wondered…why he left without even telling me goodbye."

"Your father, you mean?"

She nodded, knowing she didn't have to explain to Heath. "But let's not get into that."

"Okay." He set down his cup, then pulled her back against him on the cold blue vinyl sofa. "But can I say something?"

She nodded, burrowed her head against the warmth of his cotton shirt.

"I'm not going to leave you, Mariel. I've decided I want to be wherever you are."

Mariel couldn't look at him. Her heart escalated into a wobbly beat. "Why?"

His arms tightened around her. "Because from the moment I saw you standing there on the edge of the lilies, I knew I had to make you mine."

"Are you sure you aren't just caught up in Granny's matchmaking scheme?"

"If I am, then I like being tangled."

She felt his smile. And sank against the warmth of his touch. "She needs all of us now. A heart attack. Bypass surgery. And all she asked for… She only wanted her family around her for Easter."

"She's going to be okay," Heath said, his hand stroking Mariel's hair.

"But you can't promise me that."

"No. I just know that Sadie has accepted that she might not make it."

Mariel shot up, started pacing. "Well, I haven't accepted it. I want her home and safe. I want her standing in her kitchen, baking tea cakes and making lemonade. I want…I want…so many things." Closing her eyes, she fought tears and her own glaring insecurities. "I finished the painting—I was going to give it to her on Easter Sunday.''

She felt him beside her. "I can't promise that Sadie won't die," he said, his arms around her. "But I do know God is watching over your family. And you have Sadie to thank for that."

Mariel lifted her head. "So you believe that her faith will be strong enough for all of us?"

"Yes, I do. Her faith will carry her home, healed, into the arms of the Lord."

"I'm not ready to give her over to Him yet."

Heath held a finger to her chin. "Well, then, that's where your own faith will have to come in. You have a portrait of your grandmother, but...you've also found what's important again. You can stop spinning, Mariel."

Mariel's heart felt as if it were in a tug-of-war. "Will you be here, if the worst happens? Will you help me?"

"Yes." He nodded, kissed her tears away. "That I *can* promise."

A couple of days later, Mariel walked out of ICU to find her mother standing in the hallway with a tall, tan-skinned man. Evelyn looked up, her eyes laced with a wild fear. "Mariel?"

"What's wrong?" Mariel asked, her gaze flying from her mother's face to the man beside her. "Is something wrong with Granny—something the doctors didn't tell us?"

"No, no," Evelyn replied in a strained voice. She glanced at the man. "This is your father."

Mariel had to reach for the nearby wall railing. Leaning back against the sturdy wood, she stared at the man who'd walked out of her life all those years ago. Vincent Evans looked gaunt, a thin pallor showing clearly through his olive complexion. His hair, once dark brown, was now tinged with streaks of gray. But his eyes were a vivid blue-green, and right now, they looked misty.

"What do you want?" Mariel asked, her voice raspy.

"I—I wanted to see you," Vincent said. "Your mother and I—we ran into each other in the cafeteria downstairs. We've been talking for hours."

"I told him about Jeffrey," Evelyn said.

"That's nice."

Evelyn touched an arm to Mariel's sleeve. "Vincent and I have made our peace, Mariel. At last." She almost smiled, but Mariel saw the old pain cresting in her eyes.

"Am I supposed to be happy about that?"

"I'd like you to…consider it," Evelyn replied. "And I think you need to listen to what your father has to say."

Mariel watched as Evelyn headed for the double doors of the ICU. The swishing of those doors sounded like wind over flowers. Then there was only silence.

"What do you want?" she asked her father again.

She heard the shuffling of his feet, heard a soft, trembling sigh. "I love you," he said. Then he turned to leave.

"So…that's it?" she called after him. "You love me, and yet, you're leaving again?"

He turned, his hands in the pockets of his khaki work breeches. "I don't want to leave. I want to get to know you."

"Better late than never?"

"Yes," he said, coming back to stand in front of her. "Sadie told me you were home. Sadie said better *now*, than never."

Tears pricked at Mariel's eyes. Her grandmother had just said almost the very same words to her. "Let Heath love you, Mariel. Better to take a chance now, than never at all."

"Granny is very sick. She wants everything neat and tidy—"

"She's right to want that. I don't want her to…pass on…thinking I didn't love you."

"That's very thoughtful."

"I'm not being thoughtful. I'm being honest." When Mariel didn't respond, he said, "You Hillsboro women—always stubborn to the end."

Mariel thought about her mother, about the change that had come over Evelyn. That her parents had held a civil conversation was a miracle in itself. Maybe it was time for her to start trusting again. Sadie would tell her to use faith as her guide. *Help me, Lord.* Mariel heard the silent plea inside her head. Then she turned to face her father. "I do need some answers."

He nodded, cleared his throat. "Let's go get a cup of coffee."

Easter morning dawned in bright hues of watercolor pinks and yellows, reminding Mariel of tiny chicks and brightly painted eggs. Unable to sleep, she'd gotten up to stare at her grandmother's finished portrait just as the first rays of light had come over the eastern horizon. Now, in a floral sundress, she stood at the edge of the lily field, searching for that one perfect fully opened blossom that would herald Easter's coming. She wanted to take Sadie a fresh cutting.

Mariel listened as she stood.

So much had happened in the month she'd been home. Her mother had found a new life, while her grandmother had almost died. Her uncles had found some humility, and their children had rediscovered their precious grandmother. One of her aunts had held tight—Aunt Dee being pragmatic and loving as always—and one of her aunts had finally let go, Aunt Bree becoming more compassionate and civil. Mariel had found her passion for painting again, and had found forgiveness in her heart for her father, too.

And...Mariel had fallen in love.

She could see that now. She could see this plan had been set in motion the minute she'd seen Heath standing there in the lily field. She loved him. She didn't understand this love, but she accepted it.

And now, she stood, waiting, watching, hoping, for a sign, an answer to the dilemma that was her mixed-up life.

"You're here," she heard Heath say as he hurried up to her. "You're here."

"Where else would I be?" she asked, her words breathless with knowing.

"I don't know—I thought maybe you'd leave."

She saw the awe in his eyes, saw the love and tenderness in his smile. "I can't leave now. Granny will be home soon. She needs me."

"*I* need you," he told her as he tugged her up the path. "And I want to give you something."

Mariel hesitated, still searching for that one perfect lily to cut and take to her grandmother's hospital room. That one perfect lily to show her that God was truly watching over her.

Heath pulled her into the shed beside the gift shop. "I've had this for a week now. I planned on giving it to you on Palm Sunday."

"We were supposed to have a date that night."

"Uh-huh." His white shirt glistened in the muted early-morning light as he whirled around. "This is for you."

Mariel's gaze moved over the exquisite white flower he held up to her. "That's not an Easter Lily."

"No." He gave her that little half smile. "This is a Casablanca lily, very rare and very delicate. But they do grow in Louisiana. I wanted you to have this—to start your own lily field."

Mariel took the potted lily, sniffed its rich scent. "Heath, it's beautiful."

He stood there, his hands in the pockets of his jeans, his eyes an early-morning-sky blue. "You know, Mariel, some lilies have to be nurtured and forced to bloom."

She moved her head. "I understand."

He stepped closer. "And then, there are the wild lilies

that grow at random—part of the beauty of God's world—his gift to us.''

''They take longer to bloom sometimes,'' she said, wondering what he was trying to say.

''That's right. We have to be patient and wait for them.''

''And they don't last forever.''

''But we cherish them when they're here.''

''Which kind is this?'' she asked, touching a finger to the ruffled petals.

''Well, now, that's up to you.'' He took the lily from her, pulled her close. ''I want you to take all the time you need. And when you come to me, I want you to be in full bloom. I want you to be sure.''

''How can I know?'' she asked, the gentle whisper sounding like a plea.

''Trust, Mariel. Trust in yourself, trust in me, but especially, trust in God.''

She pulled away. ''Heath, about the lilies—I don't know if I can listen.''

''Will you try, for me?'' Then he turned away to stare at the brilliant white flower sitting there. ''Or have you already made up your mind to leave?''

Mariel knew the answer to that question, but her heart was afraid to speak it. So she turned and ran…out into the lily field. Just as she'd done when she was a child. As she ran, she remembered hearing the rustle of the sweet stalks moving against her legs, remembered the whisper of the blooming, trumpet-shaped blossoms as they splashed out into the wind.

And she remembered something else, too. She remembered the Bible lesson from Luke her grandmother had taught in Sunday school on an Easter morning long ago. The last Easter Mariel had shared with both her mother and father.

''He called her by name,'' Granny had said. ''The Lord said 'Mary.' And then Mary Magdalene knew it was Him there in the garden. Our Father had left the tomb where they had taken Him after He was crucified. He had risen.''

Mariel stopped running, her heart pounding to a steady rhythm. She stopped…and she listened.

And she remembered. ''One day, Mariel, you'll hear the Lord calling. He will call you by name, too. And then you will give your heart to His care and follow Him always.''

Mariel's hand came to her mouth as tears fell down her face. The wind lifted through the tall, elegant lilies. The breeze whispered her name.

Mariel looked up, her eyes scanning the vast, sloping field. Brilliant piercing rays of sunlight glistened off the dew on the lilies, making it look as if the lush petals were crying.

Mariel cried, too. She remembered coming here, running through this field, after she'd found out her parents were getting a divorce, after she'd found out she had been the only reason they'd married.

And on that day, she'd hid away here among the lilies.

But she remembered hearing that sweet voice, calling to her on the wings of the snow-white flowers.

''Mariel.''

Had it been the wind, calling her name? Or her grandmother, searching for her? Or had it been her own hurting heart, seeking out God's mercy and grace?

Mariel looked around now, her heart, like a new blooming flower, bursting with overwhelming memories. Somehow, she'd found comfort here that day so long ago. She hadn't been alone back then. God had been right here with her.

And He was here now.

As she stood, she saw the blossoms bending toward her, understood at last what being resurrected was all about. And she understood the powerful significance of these beautiful flowers. At last, she could hear their message lifting out on the morning breeze.

She looked up to find Heath coming toward her. Without

a word, she ran to meet him. Breathless, she said, "I listened, Heath. I heard the lilies calling my name. It sounds crazy, but I heard the Lord, telling me it would be all right."

Heath's smile was like the first rays of the sun.

"It will be all right, Mariel. I promise." Then he pulled her into his arms and kissed her. "I love you."

Mariel lifted away, touched a hand to his face. "I love you, too. I was afraid, but not anymore."

"So you'll stay?"

She leaned into him. "How could I ever leave now?" Holding him tight, she said, "I have to plant my lily. We need to start our own garden."

Heath wiped at the tears streaming down her face. "That takes time, sweetheart. Are you sure?"

"I'm sure. And I can be patient," she replied. "I think it will be worth the wait."

He grinned. "And in the meantime…we can work on getting married and…maybe starting a family?"

"That sounds wonderful," Mariel said. Then she took his hand and pulled him back toward the house. "Let's go tell Granny. I'm going to take her the portrait and an armful of lilies. She has to get well, so she can spoil her great-grandchildren."

"She's going to be so happy," Heath said.

Together they ran through the field.

The sound of their laughter lifted out over the field, while all around them, the lily petals opened to the light of a new beginning.

THE BUTTERFLY GARDEN
Gail Gaymer Martin

In memory of my grandfather John Schulert,
who loved gardening and now enjoys the garden
in heaven.

Thanks to orthopedic surgeon Gregory Zemenick.

If you have faith as small as a mustard seed,
you can say to this mountain, "Move from
here to there," and it will move.

—Matthew 17:20

Chapter One

Emily Casale's wheelchair bumped forward and jarred into the table. A splash of orange juice sprayed over her shoulder and showered her hand.

"Oops. Sorry," a masculine voice said behind her.

Emily shifted in her chair and focused on the man with the sheepish expression. He held a plate of pancakes and sausage while orange juice dripped from his fingers.

"It's not you. It's this cumbersome chair," she said.

"Not at all. I wasn't looking where I was going. I had my mind focused on my empty stomach and these pancakes." His gaze lowered to her dampened hand. "I didn't mean to douse you with juice."

He flashed her a smile. "Is this seat taken?" A chuckle followed his question. "That is, if you trust me not to do any more damage."

She couldn't help but grin. "No. The seat's empty, and I'd advise you to set that stuff down before you baptize someone else." She lifted her napkin from her lap and wiped the sticky liquid from her fingers.

She liked his smile—full with elongated dimples that

brightened his face, but his eyes were what really caught her attention. Eyes as pale blue as a winter sky.

He set down his dishes and sat in the chair adjacent to Emily's spot at the end of the table.

"Beautiful Easter morning," he said, unfolding the paper napkin and lowering it to his lap.

"Yes. It is." Emily avoided eye contact and grasped her fork. She sliced off a section of pancake, overwhelmed by the rush of anxiety that raced through her. So much time had passed since she'd spoken to an attractive man—a man who caused her pulse to skip.

She'd started out in a bad mood, coerced into coming to church. Though she loved worship, especially the Easter service, going anywhere in her wheelchair seemed like too much trouble. Nothing felt the same anymore. And strangers. She hated their looks of curiosity and pity...and their questions. But this man's eyes only smiled.

"Could you pass the coffee, please?" he asked.

Emily grasped the carafe and handed it to him, evading his gaze.

"I'm sorry," he said, holding the container poised in the air. "I didn't introduce myself." He extended his free hand. "Greg Zimmerman."

Clutching his fingers, Emily felt some distress at her jogging pulse. "Emily Casale," she said, releasing his firm grip and gesturing beside her. "This is my sister, Martha Burton."

"Marti, please," Emily's sister said. "Are you a newcomer to Unity Church?"

Greg poured coffee from the pot and returned the carafe to the table. "I moved here a couple of months ago." He glanced over his shoulder as if hoping to avoid detection, then lowered his voice. "But I've only been to two services...though I can come up with some mighty good excuses." He lifted his fork and took a bite of sausage.

Emily liked his cheerfulness. "What brought you here today? Easter or the smell of sausage?"

Greg lifted a napkin and wiped his mouth. "The sausage for sure, and doesn't everyone go to church on Easter?" His dimples gave a wink. "But to be honest, Pastor Ben made a visit and...you know. Here I am." He fingered his cup handle, then lifted it to his lips.

Emily understood. Pastor Ben had visited with her so many times since the accident and her husband's death— praying with her, encouraging her, reminding her that God walked beside her every day.

But that was the trouble. God walked. She couldn't.

"We're glad you joined us," Marti said. "Do you live nearby?"

Greg lowered the coffee cup. "Pretty close. I bought a Colonial over on Sunset in Lathrup Village."

"Sunset." Emily had spoken before she could monitor her surprise.

"You know the street?" Greg asked.

"Marti and I live on Sunset." A wave of heat rolled up her collar.

"Really. We must be neighbors."

Neighbors. Emily prayed he wasn't one of those friendly people who wanted to stop by to give her a helping hand. She wanted no one's sympathy. "So what's your new job?" she asked, anxious to change the subject to something more distant.

"I'm a physical therapist at Beaumont Hospital."

Emily's stomach plummeted. Physical therapist. She'd had her fill of them five years ago after the car accident. She didn't care about walking after her husband's death, but Marti...and the therapists had pushed her until she walked again. But now things had changed. She could no longer walk any distance without pain.

"Beaumont," Marti said. "That's close. I work in Southfield over on Telegraph. That's not bad, either."

Emily found herself pulling away from the conversation. Memories took her back to the work she loved. She'd been a horticulturist at Bordine's, a popular greenhouse. All day she would wallow in flowers and the rich scent of soil. Following Ted's death, her inability to garden had proven her second worst loss.

Adding a sentence or two to their conversation, Emily finished her breakfast and felt relieved when Greg excused himself. She found him too appealing for her own good. Marti returned their dishes to the kitchen. Then she and Emily headed toward the sanctuary.

When she settled in a front transept that allowed room for the wheelchair, Emily breathed in the rich scent of lilies. A huge wooden cross on the chancel had been filled with pots of the lovely flowers while others adorned the windowsills. The stained-glass scenes spread their pastel hues over the lilies, creating a spectrum of color.

Joyous Easter music filled the sanctuary from the organ's pipes in the balcony. Emily's irritation with Marti for insisting she come soon faded. The music roused her spirit, and Greg-the-baptizer's pale blue eyes warmed her thoughts.

From her vantage point, Emily looked into the congregation and spotted Greg near the front. His short, neat hair, brown with a few gray highlights, looked attractive. She guessed him to be in his late thirties.

To keep herself from ogling, she opened the church bulletin and read through the list of lily donors, her name among them. "Emily Casale, in loving memory of her husband, Ted."

With sadness, Emily realized that Ted had truly become a memory. Details of their life together had melded into categories of bright and difficult moments…like all marriages, she assumed. If she'd been the one to die in the accident, would Ted have remained unmarried all these years? She doubted it. He needed companionship and someone to handle the responsibilities. She'd been honored if he had mowed the lawn without her prodding. Still, she grinned at the memory.

The organ prelude melded into the opening hymn, and the congregation rose. Instinctively, Emily pushed her hands against the chair arms to rise, then let them slip to her lap in defeat.

Forcing herself away from self-pity, she opened the hymnal and joined in the rousing hymn. Maybe she couldn't walk, but she could sing.

The service continued with the Easter message, and during the offering, to avoid staring at Greg, her gaze settled on the beautiful new Easter banners that hung on each side of the chancel—glorious butterflies with colorful wings.

Emily pictured the butterflies flitting among her flowers, and she yearned for the past—to enjoy her garden and to be free like those fragile creatures.

She focused again on the butterfly banners. Against a white background was written four words—From Death to Life. *Death.* Many times she'd asked herself why she had lived and Ted had died. Sometimes her life seemed like death...only in a different form. Poor me, she yelled into her thoughts. She wanted no part of self-pity. Yet it continued to surface.

Her eyes shifted from the lovely banners to Greg, and she caught him looking back at her. A mixture of embarrassment and pleasure spiraled through her chest.

She looked away as the congregation rose for the final song while an intriguing thought entered her mind. Though they'd been at breakfast for nearly an hour, Greg had never asked her why she was in a wheelchair.

Clasping her hymnal as the organ swelled with the introduction, Emily lifted her hymnal and let her spirit ride on the surging melody. "I Know That My Redeemer Lives." The song had always been her favorite. She rejoiced as voices soared into the vaulted ceiling. "He lives. He lives who once was dead." Would she ever live again? The question burdened her mind.

When the song ended, parishioners closed the hymnals and made their way down the aisles.

"Wonderful service," Marti said, placing her songbook in the pew rack.

"It was. Thanks for insisting I come," Emily said, niggled by remorse at her negative attitude that morning.

"You're welcome." A tender look spread across her sister's face. "I'll run and pick up the lily."

Emily remained where she had been through the service, and in a moment, Marti returned carrying a potted lily, placed it in Emily's arms, then guided the chair to the vestibule doorway.

A handicap ramp led outside, and Emily drew in a deep breath of the pungent spring air. As if the day were blessed, sunshine had turned the sky a gorgeous cerulean blue and heated the budding flower beds, sending the lush scent of warmed earth mingled with the lily nestled in her arms. New growth. New life. New hope. And wasn't that the meaning of Easter? The thought made her smile.

"Wonderful service, wasn't it?"

Emily turned and looked into Greg's friendly face. The sunlight flooded his eyes and he squinted.

"Very nice," she said.

He raised his arm and shielded his eyes. In his free hand, he carried a lily. "The floral cross is unique. I've never seen anything like it."

He must have noticed her looking at the flower because he answered her unspoken question.

In a casual gesture, he hiked up the plant. "The lily's

for my mother…in memory of my dad. I'm taking it over there later today.''

"That's nice," Emily said. "I'm sure she'll like it."

"My mom's a flower fanatic. As soon as the weather warms up, she spends all day in the garden."

Emily winced—her own yearning fresh and aching.

"If you want to see a beautiful display," Marti said, "you need to stop by. Emily has an amazing garden."

Emily's pulse pumped. She had to stop Marti. "I did have…once." She focused on her damaged legs. "My dahlias have all died, and, it's too early for most flowers. Not much is in bloom yet."

"I'd like to see it sometime," Greg said, still shielding his eyes.

"If you have time now, drop by for coffee…unless you're in a hurry," Marti said. "Our house must be very close to yours."

Emily cringed at her sister's blatant matchmaking. Marti certainly wasn't inviting Greg for her own interest. She'd been engaged for the past year and, to Emily, her sister's wedding loomed on the calendar like a prison sentence. Not that she wasn't happy for her, but Emily had no idea how she could live alone without Marti. Not her money— Emily had been receiving disability. Emily needed her companionship and help.

"I'm in no hurry," Greg said. "I'd like to stop by."

If Emily could swing her leg around the chair, she would have kicked her sister in the shin.

Greg settled in the Casale living room, amazed that they lived only three houses from his own on the other side of the street. Small world, he thought.

Though Marti had been gracious with her invitation, Greg sensed Emily hadn't been thrilled with her sister's offer. In fact, at the church, Greg had watched Marti ma-

neuver Emily's wheelchair into the car and had wanted to
volunteer his help, but he'd perceived the offer wouldn't
be appreciated by Emily. It wasn't what she said, but
rather, the look in her eye. A look that said, "Don't help
and don't ask."

And he hadn't.

But his career as a physical therapist awakened his desire to ask her about her diagnosis and prognosis. With
technology today, many people could be walking again if
they only had faith in medical advances.

Emily was an attractive woman—witty and sharp—but
what drew him was her vulnerability.

"Here we are," Marti said, pushing Emily's chair across
the plush carpet while Emily held a tray. The thick pile
caused the wheels to sink into the nap. He saw Marti's
struggle and jumped up to help her.

She gave him a grateful look, and he placed the chair
beside a table, then pulled on the brake. When he stepped
away, sadness filled Emily's face, but Greg ignored it and
chattered on about the fragrance of the coffee and the de-
licious-looking cake.

When he had settled in the chair, Marti doled out the
treats. Greg sipped coffee and enjoyed the apple torte, turning the conversation to the church and to anything other
than Emily's condition. Still, he knew the topic had to
come up before he left.

Emily released a frustrated sigh, stretching toward the
table with her empty plate.

Rising, Marti took the plate from her hand. "Emily
wouldn't be in that chair if she'd see a specialist."

Emily shot her a fiery glare. "Marti, please, this isn't
the time to talk about our family matters."

Marti's expression drooped, and she lowered her head
as if hurt by her sister's words.

Greg swallowed the questions that boiled in his head

and offered a calming comment. "I'm sure it's hard on your sister to see you bound to a wheelchair. I'd feel the same way if you were my sister."

Emily looked at him with contrition. "I know. I just lose patience sometimes." She shifted toward her sister. "Marti, I'm sorry to have snapped."

Marti nodded, remaining silent while her hurt expression faded.

Giving in to his curiosity, Greg took a careful step forward. "How long have you been in the chair, Emily?"

"About eight months. I can walk a little. A few steps, but it's painful."

Bravely, Greg forged ahead. "What happened?"

"Arthritis." She looked out the window as if afraid to look in his eyes. "Complications and arthritis."

"Complications…from an accident?"

She nodded. "Five years ago my husband was killed in a rollover accident on the Southfield Freeway. My legs were crushed."

"She did really well," Marti said. "Within a year, she was back to normal…walking."

The "back to normal" comment hadn't hit Emily well. Her face said more than her words.

"That must have been a very difficult time for you."

"It was." She let her hands slip from the chair arms and clutched them in her lap, her tension obvious. "I try to find something positive in tragedy. Spending so much time learning to walk again helped me to heal from my husband's death."

Greg wanted to comment on what she said. He wanted to praise her for looking for the positive side of a horrible situation, but he feared the compliment would come off as patronizing.

"Being in the business," he said, settling for a different

direction, "I know how difficult therapy can be. It takes a lot of fortitude and courage. You certainly have that."

She raised her eyes slowly to his as if surprised at the compliment. "Thanks, but I had a lot of prodding." She tilted her head toward Marti.

"Well, then, praise God for sisters."

His comment caused her to chuckle and Greg was encouraged by her smile. Not wanting to make her any more uneasy, Greg rose and placed his dishes on the tray. "So, when do I see this famous garden?"

Emily shook her head. "You'll be disappointed. You should have waited until May when the flowers are in full bloom."

"I can come back then, too. I only live across the street." He sent her a grin, hoping she'd smile back.

She didn't.

He rubbed his hands together. "Do you have a ramp in back or just the one in front?"

"In back, too," Marti said. "I'll let you have the honors while I take care of these dishes." She grasped the tray and hurried from the room.

"Ready?" Greg asked.

Emily nodded and put her hand on the wheel of her chair, but it didn't budge. "I'm just not strong enough to be imprisoned in this thing."

Greg bit his tongue. She didn't have to be in that "thing," as she called it. Surgery worked miracles.

"Let me push," he said. "I've got muscles from forcing my patients to do untold torturous exercises."

She laughed. "And that's why I refuse to see a specialist."

He let the thought drop and remained silent while he pushed her past Marti, then down the porch ramp to the backyard.

"You can park me on the driveway. It'll be easier." She motioned for him to go toward the garden.

He did as she said and wandered across the spongy lawn. He understood why she loved her garden. Tall thickets followed the fence, creating a private, lush backdrop. Scattered amid the shade trees and sunny spots, she had cultivated areas, some enclosed by sculpted shrubs. Between the flower beds, stepping stones wound through the lawn, forming a path decked with a birdbath, garden benches and even a sundial. Unique, like a secluded park.

"It's beautiful, Emily." He turned to face her. "I can see why you miss getting out here."

A look of nostalgia flooded her face. "It took more than three years to get it like this. Trimming, weeding, mulching. It's pretty much gone to seed."

He felt himself losing control. She was a lovely woman—good-humored, beautiful…with her misty green eyes, copper-colored hair cropped like a pixie and with so much life to live. "You have a lot of blossoms coming up. I'm sure it's still beautiful in the summer."

"It used to be." Her gaze drifted to flower beds. "It's my butterfly garden." Her voice heartened.

An image of the church banners popped into his thoughts. From Death to Life.

"Butterfly garden? What's that?" he asked.

"Flowers that lure butterflies."

Greg chuckled. "I didn't know I could lure a butterfly." As the words left him, he was struck by a greater meaning.

"You can. Yes." Emily shifted in her chair, her face glowing with enthusiasm. "Black-eyed Susans, asters, lavender, oxeye daisies, purple coneflowers, coreopsis, even butterfly weed. And look." She pointed to a cluster of trees in the far corner of the yard. "And lilacs."

"You plant the flowers and then the butterflies show up," he said.

She drew in a lengthy breath and nodded. "Yes. Can you think of anything more beautiful…or free?"

Yes. He could….

Emily's summer garden filled his imagination—bright colors tossing in the breeze with ethereal butterflies fluttering among the blossoms.

And Emily…as beautiful, but not free.

Chapter Two

Greg Zimmerman slipped off his hospital smock and pulled a windbreaker from his locker. Shrugging it on as he walked, he headed for the exit.

All day his mind had been filled with Emily. Why would she want to spend her life in a wheelchair if she didn't have to? He'd seen vestiges of her self-pity and avoidance, determined to fight surgery. But why? He knew enough about damaged limbs to be confident her situation could be rectified.

His thoughts turned to his own stored self-pity. For years he'd avoided emotions that stabbed at him when he thought of his brother, Aaron, the child's twisted limbs—but then, he could do nothing.

As he stepped outside, he noted the air hinted of an early summer. He climbed into his SUV, feeling uplifted. The warm, balmy weather brought images of growth and re-birth to mind.

Greg rested his elbows on the steering wheel. He entwined his fingers and propped his chin on his hands, closing his eyes to his own memories. Emily's pale, sun-starved face slid back into his mind. What could he do to sway this young woman to take a leap of faith?

An idea burst into his thoughts.

Motivated by his brainstorm, Greg turned the key in the ignition and pulled away from the parking lot. Traveling down the tree-lined highway, he eyed the greening leaves and along the path, new grass poked above the winter-brown blades.

Everything died eventually, then taking new roots, was born again. Leaves, grass, flowers, even God's children. Dead to the world, but rooted in the Word, they were re-born in heaven.

It happened on earth, too. Hopes and dreams might die, but rooted in faith, new ideas and fresh aspirations could blossom to reality. That's what he wanted for Emily Casale. She'd snagged his interest and he longed to see her bloom again.

As Greg turned the corner, the familiar white bungalow appeared. He parked in the driveway and climbed the porch steps. Before he reached the door, it opened.

"Greg, what a nice surprise."

"I know, Mom. It's been over a week since Easter Sunday. Time gets away from me." Guilt nudged his conscience.

"I don't expect you to hover over me." Her grin brightened her powdery complexion. "Come in. I hope you have time to visit."

He stepped inside, gave her a hug and followed her into the living room. "I even have enough time for—"

"Dinner, I hope."

"You read my mind."

"Good. Mothers are supposed to do that. And my mother's instinct tells me you have something else on your mind."

The twinkle in her eye caused him to chuckle. He

rubbed his neck. "I never could get anything over on you."

"It's those telling eyes. You'd open your mouth and spill out everything before I had to ask." Like old times, she stood by the doorway, waiting.

"You expect me to spill everything before I eat?" He sniffed the air. "So what's on the menu? Roast beef?"

"Grind it up, and you've got it. Meat loaf."

Her chuckle lingered on the air as he followed her into the kitchen.

While his mother stood at the sink, mashing potatoes, Greg ambled to the sliding patio door and looked out into the backyard. Yellow daffodils and colorful tulips stood above the dark earth, and peeking from the moist loam, summer flowers forced their way into the light. Like Emily—life below the surface, waiting to leap into the sunshine.

"Something interesting out there?"

Greg turned back to the kitchen. "No. Just thinking about your garden."

"Everything's ready, I think." She placed a bowl of buttered fresh green beans on the table and patted a chair.

He joined her at the table, and following the blessing, he filled his plate with the homemade bounty. "I need a woman in my life just like you."

"You mean a gray-haired lady who likes to cook?"

"I wouldn't go that far."

She patted his hand and paused as if the counseling session had begun. "So what's on your mind?"

He lifted a forkful of meat loaf. "This isn't about me, Mom, so you can wipe that know-it-all expression off your face. I want to talk about a disabled woman who loves gardening."

He knew he had disappointed her as evidenced by her

creased forehead. She'd wanted to hear about a woman in his life.

"A patient?" she asked. "Now that I hadn't considered."

"No, not a patient."

"But a woman, you said."

An uncomfortable heat edged up his collar. Gaining time, he drank from his water glass. "Yes. A woman."

"Aah."

"No. Not 'aah.' She's a member of Unity Church. Young and in a wheelchair...and determined to stay there."

"Why?"

A frown pulled at his mouth and he shook his head. "I have no idea. She's frightened, I think. I don't know. But I'd like to pry her out of that chair."

"Must have some reason for wanting to stay there." She ate a bite and gazed into the distance. "So how can I help?"

"She mentioned dahlias. You grow them, right?"

"I do. Such a beautiful flower."

Like Emily, he thought. "I'd like to give her some seeds. You know, something to encourage her into her garden again."

"Try tubers." A grin spread across her face. "Dahlias are from tubers, not seeds."

"You see. That's why I need your help. You can tell me what I need to know."

"About the dahlias...or about women?"

"Mushy peas," Emily said with a glare, sitting in the passenger seat beside Marti, her arms folded across her chest.

"What?"

"Remember when we were kids and Mom forced us to

eat those gray-green peas because she said they were good for us? That's exactly what you're doing.''

Marti slapped her palm against the steering wheel and shook her head. ''We've been over it and over it, Emily. If you want to think of me as shoving peas down your throat then think it.''

Stray tears escaped Emily's eyes and ran like an insult down her cheek. To catch the culprits, she unwound her arms momentarily and wiped the dampness with her fingers. She then bound her arms again like a tourniquet against her chest. ''It all boils down to my ruining your life. And I suppose I do.''

''If you want to wallow in self-pity, go ahead. But you heard what the surgeon said. You'll walk again if you have the surgery.'' She pinned Emily with her gaze.

Marti pulled into their driveway and stepped from the car. She closed the driver's door and circled to the rear.

Emily faced the house and watched Marti in the side mirror, her face marred by a frown—a frown Emily had put there.

The passenger door swung open, and Marti guided the wheelchair close to Emily.

''Now, be careful.'' She locked the brakes and stood behind the chair, holding it in place.

''How many times have I crawled into this thing?'' Emily snapped, but with the words, reality slapped her stinging tongue to silence. That was the point, and she knew it. How long had she sat in the wheelchair? Eight months? Nearly a year? And Marti had moved in and cared for her without complaint.

Marti grabbed Emily's purse from the front seat, dropped it on her lap and slammed the car door. In silence, she pushed the chair along the sidewalk.

''Did you see the surgeon today?''

Emily's head pivoted and saw Greg walking up the sidewalk behind them, carrying a paper bag.

"Don't ask," Marti said, giving him an eye-rolling look.

Greg grinned. "Okay. But let me take over for you." He stepped beside Marti and took over the handles of the chair. "It's too nice to go inside. What do you say?"

Emily lifted her gaze to the promising blue sky. She drew in a refreshing breath. One of the things she loved about Michigan was the changing seasons, and spring always held promises. "I suppose."

"Let's go out back. I have a present for you."

She looked at him over her shoulder. "A present?"

He lifted the paper sack for a moment, then returned his hand to the chair. "It's not gift-wrapped, but it's a gift…from my mother."

"Your mother?" "Why?" and "What?" whirred in her head, and it gave her an uneasy feeling.

In a moment, he stopped her chair and pulled on the brake, then set the sack in her lap.

"I don't understand." She gazed at him, then at the gift. "What is it?"

"Look inside." He sat beside her on a garden bench.

Cautiously, she unwound the top and peeked into the opening. "Dahlias." A lump formed in her throat, and she dug down into the sack and pulled out a handful of dahlia tubers. No matter how hard she swallowed, her emotion bubbled into her eyes.

"My mom has flower beds," he said, his voice as tender as a mother to her child. "She thought you'd like these."

His gaze penetrated her heart. "But…how does your mother know that I love dahlias?"

He faltered. "You mentioned it the other day. I told her you liked them, and she sent you some roots."

Touched by their thoughtfulness, Emily's tears won the

battle. They rolled down her cheeks and dripped on the earth-dusted tubers in her palm.

"I didn't mean to upset you," he said, his voice like the brush of a feather.

Emily shook her head. "Tell her thank you," she said. "I'm sure they'd be beautiful if—"

"They are beautiful. They just need to be put in the ground."

What could she say? If he only knew she thought about it often. That and so many things.

"If you put those back in the bag, you can use this to wipe the dirt off your hands." He pulled his handkerchief from his back pocket and handed it to her.

Emily lowered the tubers into the sack and Greg traded her—the sack for his hankie. She brushed the dust from her fingers, then handed it back. "Thanks."

"I know you don't want to talk about it, but I'm still going to ask. What did he say?"

"Who?" She knew full well what he meant, but she felt like being stubborn.

He didn't answer her, and after a long silence, she gave in. "I'm bone on bone. Surgery's a must or I'll sit in this chair for the rest of my life." She waited for his rebuttal.

He only looked at her, his eyes filled with tenderness.

"Where's my lecture?" she asked.

"It's your decision, but in my work, I've seen too many people walk again who thought their world had ended. That's what'll happen to you. You'll walk again."

She knew that, but the problem was deeper. She couldn't open her soul to a man she barely knew. "It's not that easy. There's pain, therapy, possible blood clots." And loneliness.

"Sure. And I could get hit by a truck, crossing the road."

Greg, Marti and the world. No one understood. She

pulled a brochure from her pocket—one the surgeon had given her to read—and handed it to him.

"This is what I'm supposed to think about."

Taking the brochure. Greg glanced over the pages without comment. Emily realized he understood. He worked with patients who'd gone through all kinds of surgery and reconstruction...but it was different when the surgery was your own.

He closed the pamphlet, and his gaze drifted to her face. Without words, she read so much in his eyes.

"I realize Marti needs a life of her own," Emily said. The words tore at her. A reality, yet leaving her burdened with fear and solitude.

He nodded. "How old is Marti?"

"Thirty-one." Thirty-one and still waiting for marriage. Guilt weighted against her heart.

"I'm surprised she's still single. You've really been blessed with her company."

He had no idea what thoughts raced through her mind. "Marti's been engaged for over a year. Her wedding is in December."

"December?" His eyes widened beneath lifted brows.

Emily realized she'd startled him...and embarrassed him after his previous comment. "I understand why she's pressuring me to get this done, but I can manage on my own, and what I can't do, I'll hire someone to help me."

He didn't comment, but she saw his hand touch the paper bag filled with dahlia tubers.

Emily drew in a quick breath. "I can walk short distances. I just can't carry anything. You know, a laundry basket or grocery bags. But if I hire someone to help, then Marti and Randy can get married and that's that." She felt her chin jut forward like a belligerent child, and she tucked it back.

"Pretty determined, aren't you?" He rose and handed

her the brochure. "This brochure explains it all. Every detail. All you have to do is—"

She flexed her palm toward him. "Don't say it. I've heard it all before."

Drawing in a deep breath, he wondered. Maybe it was more than the surgery. She was lovely, yet terribly vulnerable…the way he felt as he was growing up. He'd suffered with so many feelings. Guilt over Aaron's death. Sorrow that it wasn't he who died instead of his little brother. He saw his own despair reflected in Emily's eyes.

"I've never heard you so quiet," Emily said, her voice breaking the lengthy silence.

"Thinking."

"I didn't mean to interrupt."

Her playful quip made him grin. "I think quite often, actually. Not always wisely, but I do think." The situation of the moment came to mind, and his pulse tripped up his arms. "I was giving thought to a meeting I have tonight." A two-hundred-watt lightbulb glared in his head. "You might enjoy something like that."

"Like what?"

"A meeting for the Special Olympics. I'm a volunteer. Never in my life have I felt as much pleasure as I have working with these children." Except for my feelings at this moment. He glanced her way, wondering if she sensed his interest in her.

Her gaze met his, then she shifted it toward the garden. "Must be nice."

"Have you ever seen the Special Olympics?"

"No." She continued looking past him.

"You should. Talk about enthusiasm and positive determination. Those kids are the best example of finding joy and success even when things are at their worst."

"They're all in wheelchairs…like me?"

"No. Some are, but the games are for mental disabilities, too. A tremendous organization. You'll never see such drive and energy anywhere. These kids don't give up. If they fail, they try again.''

"Kids can bounce back."

Her words settled on him slowly. "We can all bounce back if it's important enough. But we need a goal. Something to aim for. That's the secret."

She shifted her eyes toward him. "You know, before the accident I had so much energy when spring finally came. I would hurry outside, cleaning up the old growth, cultivating the soil, plotting my flower beds. I couldn't wait to get my hands into the dirt."

For the first time since he'd met her, she wanted to talk, and he let her. He settled down again on the bench and stretched out his legs. "See. You had a purpose." And now he hoped she would find a purpose again.

She nodded. "Besides this garden, I worked at a greenhouse and had my hands in soil all day. You'd think I'd have something else on my mind, but I didn't."

He grinned. "Shows you how important interests and goals are. And I suppose you've guessed that… My goal is for you to have the surgery."

He watched her smile fade. "That's obvious, but, like you said, it has to be my goal, not yours."

She straightened her back and lifted her shoulders. "I appreciate your concern. You're kind and sympathetic. I can see that."

"Empathetic," he corrected. "I understand, because I've been where you are, Emily. I still am sometimes, if I'm honest with you. I know what hopelessness and loneliness are."

Her color faded at his words. Yet a tinge of curiosity shone in her eyes. "Maybe someday you'd like to tell me why in the world you'd feel hopeless and lonely."

Chapter Three

A cold snap turned Emily's dreams of flower beds and warm days into a vague hope. She sat in the kitchen alcove, staring at the backyard. Though late April, minuscule snowflakes drifted from the sky like an afterthought, melting as soon as each lone crystal touched the ground.

But the outside chill was no more disheartening than the icy thoughts that filled her mind. The pamphlet the surgeon had given her made surgery seem like a horror movie. Plastic and metal replacing her bone and cartilage. And the restrictions and weeks of therapy and healing.

She released a stream of bound air from her lungs and grasped the coffeemaker on the table, pouring herself a fresh cup.

Noise sounded in the hallway, and she peered at the doorway as Marti strolled in with a gigantic yawn.

"I haven't slept that well in weeks." Marti eyed the wall clock and shook her head. "Ten. I'm embarrassed." She grabbed a mug from the cabinet hook and sank onto a chair.

"Don't be. You work hard. I wish I could do more, but you know I can only stand for a few—"

"Please don't apologize. I'm your sister, and I'll be here for you…as long as I can."

She lowered her eyes, and Emily knew where her thoughts were.

"So how are the wedding plans?" A rush of panic rose to Emily's chest.

"Fine," Marti said, pushing the mug in a circle in front of her. "Randy says I'm dragging my feet, but I'm not. You know how it is—menus, photographer, flowers, cake, invitations, dresses. Weddings take time to plan."

"And you're worried about me, Marti. I know you are."

"Sure, that's a given, but that's not stopping me."

"He Ain't Heavy, He's My Brother" shot through Emily's mind. At Boy's Town in Nebraska, she remembered seeing the famous statue of the older boy with a child on his shoulders.

But this was different. Marti was her younger sister. Where was Emily's support for her? And especially for her wedding. She wanted to scream. Not at Marti, but at herself.

When Emily raised her eyes, Marti was peering at her.

"Don't get morbid on me, Emily." Marti shifted her focus to the mug. She pulled the pot forward, poured, then leaned against the chair back with a look of resignation. "I suppose I should get busy. No rest for the wicked even on Saturday. I'll start the laundry, then maybe I could run out and pick up a few groceries."

Emily stared at her, not knowing what to say. And whatever she said, Marti didn't want to hear it. She wanted action.

"Can I help you work on the wedding arrangements?" Emily asked, surprising herself. "Make phone calls. I can do that. You know, get prices and details for you."

Distracted, Marti pulled herself upward, then tuned in to her sister's questioning. "I'm sorry, I was thinking."

"Phone calls. Could I help with that?"

She hesitated. Surprised? Confused?

"Sure. I have questions I want to ask the hall coordinator. No reason why you can't do that." She gulped the rest of her coffee and rose. "You know I tried to convince Randy to have a church reception. Just cake and maybe tea sandwiches. He said, 'No, you only get married once, Marti. We might as well do it up good.'"

Marti rinsed the cup and dropped it in the dishwasher. "I might as well have talked to the wall." She reached the doorway, then turned back to Emily. "I'll get the list for you. And thanks."

"No problem. It's the least I can do."

Pushing her guilt aside, Emily turned her attention to the yard, thinking of the bag of dahlia tubers that sat behind her on the kitchen counter. How much time she spent nurturing, weeding and caring for those lovely plants. And she did so much less for herself.

Unbidden, a Bible verse worked through her mind, "See how the lilies of the field grow. They do not labor or spin. Yet I tell you that not even Solomon in all his splendor was dressed like one of these…. O you of little faith."

Faith. Where had it gone? How long had it been since she asked God to lift her up or guide her path? Her path. She turned her eyes to the garden again, following the winding stepping stones through the flower beds. *Oh, Lord, give me courage. Help me to walk again.*

Emily pulled her metal walker to her side and hoisted herself to a standing position, clinging to the rubber grips and waiting for the pain to subside. "O you of little faith," she repeated in her head.

Emily met Marti in the hallway, and with the list and notepad tucked into the cloth pocket hanging from the walker, she made her way to the telephone. Easing into the cushions, she drew the phone to her side and opened the steno pad, scanning the lengthy list of questions.

No answer. Call back later. Probably too early to telephone halls, she realized finally. She rested her hand on the receiver, wondering what she should do with her time.

When the phone rang, she jumped and knocked the receiver from the hook. Chuckling at her overzealous heart, Emily pulled the receiver from the floor by the cord and put it to her ear with a hello that echoed her laughter.

"You're in a good mood."

She frowned at the receiver. "Greg?"

"None other."

His voice resounded with his own lightheartedness. She loved the natural humor in his voice. "How are you?"

"Great. What are you doing?"

She gazed down at the notebook and pencil in her lap. "I've been trying to make a call for Marti. About the wedding." Her mind raced for the reason for his call.

"Are you at work?" she asked.

He paused, making her more addled than before. "No, I'm off today. I'm calling because I'd like to take you somewhere this afternoon."

Take me somewhere? "What do you mean?"

"I mean take you somewhere. A surprise."

Her head swam. "I don't really like surprises. Plus, you've probably set up an impromptu surgery."

"You can trust me." His cheerfulness filled the line. "I'm your friend. Remember?"

His offer made her wonder. She longed to go...to do anything different. But... "Thanks, but I don't think I can today." Emily wished she could erase her response. Why had she refused?

"You have a date. Is that it?"

"A date?" Her voice raised a few decibels. "With my TV, maybe."

"There are only reruns, Emily. Come along and I'll add dinner."

Her pulse tripped up her arm. She hadn't been out with a man since Ted had died. Not even for lunch.

"I guess my invitation's taken your breath away," he said, "or did you hang up?"

She laughed at that. "I'm here. Just trying to figure out what you're up to and wondering if I play hard to get what else you'll offer me. I've always wanted to go to Hawaii."

"Can't fit that into my schedule today. But you never know."

The line hung heavy with silence while Emily scuffled for a response. Having somewhere to go on a Saturday night seemed unbelievable. "What time?"

"Did you ask what time?" His voice had brightened. "How about two?"

"Let's get this straight. This is Emily Casale. Are you sure I'm the Emily you wanted to talk with?"

Greg checked Emily's expression when they pulled into the community recreation center parking lot. He turned the steering wheel into a handicap space and hung Emily's special sticker over the rearview mirror. She didn't ask, but eyed him curiously.

He pulled the key from the ignition and opened the door. "You're in for a treat."

"You want me to run laps?" Her eyebrows rose, but a faint smile curved her lips.

"Not quite." He hadn't had this much fun in years.

When he'd gotten the wheelchair ready, she slid into it and gave him a fleeting smile to cover the pain he knew she suffered.

When they entered the facility, noise resounded from

the large gymnasium, and once through the wide double doors, a parent waved to him. Greg smiled back, feeling his heart swell as it always did when he came here.

"What is this?" Emily asked. She surveyed the room. "It's Special Olympics, right? You want me to see the kids rehearse."

"You're partly right." He clamped his teeth to avoid laughing.

"Partly? In what way?"

"We sports guys call it practice, not a rehearsal."

Her laughter warmed his heart. Her eyes sparkled while color flooded her pale cheeks framed by her short red hair. He noticed today she'd worn makeup—lipstick and mascara. She looked like a fragile flower.

He slipped off his windbreaker and hung it over a chair. "Do you mind if I help for a while? I'm a volunteer coach."

"No. That's fine. Just park me against the wall or some-place out of the way."

"You'll never be in the way, Emily."

Wheeling her to the sidelines, the pain behind her comment touched him. He set the brakes and squeezed her shoulder, then headed toward the others. He wasn't an athlete by any means, but with this group, everyone was a winner.

Emily watched him, knowing why he'd brought her here. Anger, frustration, irritation—any of the emotions might have wreaked havoc on her a week ago, but today she felt none of them. Instead, gratitude enveloped her. Whether she wanted it or not, Greg had dragged her out into the world.

"Hi."

Emily turned her head toward the voice. "Hi."

A boy, perhaps nine, stood beside her, eyeing her wheelchair. He wore a helmet and clutched a basketball under his misshapen arm.

"Can't you walk?" he asked in a thick, faltering voice.

"Not very far."

"What's wrong with you?"

Too many things, Emily might have said. "I was in an accident and hurt my legs."

"Oh," he said, dragging the word along with the turn of his head.

"Butch." A man beckoned to the child.

"He needs me," the boy said, pride in his voice. He turned and lumbered toward the coach.

He needs me. The lovely words wrapped around Emily's heart. To be needed. What more could a person want?

Though absorbed with the children, Emily was captivated by Greg. His face glowed as he demonstrated, with endless patience, how to handle the ball and the techniques for shooting a basket. Though they were limited in abilities, Emily delighted at the children's eager attempts to repeat what Greg showed them, over and over. In a rare calm moment, he flashed her a deep-dimpled grin, and for once, she felt special…like the children.

As she studied him, his muscled chest and broad shoulders rippled beneath the knit shirt as he guided them through the exercises.

Working with the children, Greg's smile seemed as generous as his spirit. Why hadn't he married and had children of his own?

Children of his own. The question startled her. She winced facing the truth. Unless God granted a miracle, she would never know such a joy.

She forced the sad thoughts from her mind, and concentrated on the action. Time flew, and when Greg returned to her, wiping his face with a towel, she laughed.

"Too much for an old man?" she asked.

"Thirty-seven's not old, is it?" he said in a quivering voice. He hunched his shoulders and clumped toward her.

But instead of staying, he squeezed her arm and excused himself. She watched him hurry off and wondered where he had gone. She hated the helpless feeling of being stranded, bound to the chair.

Within minutes, Greg reappeared, wearing a clean shirt and a ready smile. "Sorry to leave you, but I figured you'd prefer to have dinner with a man in a clean, dry shirt."

She agreed, sorry that his disappearance had caused her to feel forsaken.

By five-thirty, she was sitting at a cozy table at Mario's Italian Cuisine, staring at a menu. "Do you know how long it's been since I was invited out to dinner?"

"Too long, I'm sure."

She nodded and scanned the menu for the fifth time, longing to order a little of all her favorites. "I can't decide."

"Here's the deal. Pick one today, and I'll bring you back next week."

Pleased at his silly suggestion, she shook her head and decided. "Veal piccata," she said when the waiter took her order. When he left, she relaxed and viewed her surroundings.

"So, what did you think about the 'rehearsal?'" Greg asked, his voice teasing.

He rested his hand on the tabletop only a few inches from her own.

"Interesting."

"That's all?"

"I enjoyed watching you perspire." She shook her head. "I'm just getting even. Every time you mention surgery, I break out in a cold sweat."

He rested his hand against hers. "I don't mean to frighten you."

Fighting her instinct to draw her hand away, she eyed his fingers so close to hers. "And *you* make me nervous."

"You mean this," he asked, pressing his palm against her hand. "Or is it my talking about the surgery?"

"Both."

"I can feel you tense. I'm not trying to scare you in either way. I'd hoped today you'd see how the kids are determined and optimistic. Some have so little going for them. Only their faith."

"They are persistent. Is that where you got your persistence training?" She hoped her playful question would lighten the conversation.

"Could be. They helped me face my own self-pity…a little. Do you know what the Special Olympics' oath is?"

Emily had no idea and waited, certain he'd tell her.

"Let me win. But if I cannot win, let me be brave in the attempt."

The words settled on her like a brick. He locked his gaze to hers, and she had no escape.

"Maybe when you're young it's easier to be brave, Greg."

He gazed at her without a word.

Seeing the disappointment in his eyes, her heart wept.

Chapter Four

When the meal ended, Emily leaned back with her teacup poised in her hand. "I enjoyed dinner, but I think you have an ulterior motive."

Greg's heart gave a firm thud. Throughout the meal, he had wondered how he would present his offer and if she would accept his suggestion. He gazed at her tense face. "I wanted to make you a deal...of sorts."

"I have surgery and you do what?"

"Wrong." He watched stress vanish from her face.

"Here's the deal. You want your garden planted, and I'm willing to be your gardener if—"

"No. No. You're a therapist, not a handyman, Greg. You don't have time to do that. Thanks anyway. Marti can help...or maybe, I'll hire someone. I can sit in my chair and—"

"Hold on. Getting my hands in dirt isn't a task. You know my mother has flower beds. So guess who digs my mother's plots. Who totes the flats of flowers? Who helps water and weed?"

"You?" she asked, her face doubtful. "When would you have time for that?"

"When I'm exhausted from forcing people to exercise their arms and legs. Everyone needs a hobby. I have a couple. Special and Wheelchair Olympics, then playing in dirt. I've always enjoyed it."

"You don't seem the type."

"That's because you haven't seen all sides of me... yet." He watched her face to see her reaction. "I'm a man, Emily. Besides a career, I have a personal life like everyone else who feels, laughs, cries and loves." He slid his hand across the table and rested it on hers.

She stared at his hand before lifting misty eyes to his. "I'm sorry that I'm so...edgy. I know you're a man. One that's kind and generous. All the things a Christian should be. Compassionate and humble."

"You're pushing it there."

She ignored him and continued. "And you're patient. I'm a testimony to that. And forgiving."

"Stop. You're giving me far more credit than you should." His thoughts tugged back to Aaron's death. Eight years old. Crushed beneath car wheels, on a sled that Greg should have been riding. He had yet to forgive himself.

"Thanks for the accolades, but this is about you. I'll help in the garden if you'll help me with the Special Olympics this year."

Her forehead crinkled and her eyes narrowed with his offer. "I don't get it. What could I do, and how does that help you?"

"I'm responsible for getting volunteers for the Olympics each year. It takes a lot of people to hold the competitions in the spring. I beat the bushes asking for help—senior citizens, professional athletes, coaches, teachers, business people."

"But I'm not a professional." She grinned. "And I'm not a senior citizen yet."

"No, I'll give you that." He squeezed her fingers and withdrew his hand. "You could do lots of things. Assist with registration, greet the participants, work on telephone campaigns and mass mailings. A million jobs. Things that can be done from a wheelchair."

Though she listened, he saw suspicion in her eyes. "Okay, but I see another ulterior motive here. Admit it."

He wagged his head at her persistence. "Sure. I do have another reason. Two if I'm honest."

"I'm all for honesty."

"Good, because that's what I want from you."

He took a deep breath to quell his charging pulse. "I'd like you to spend time with children who have no possibility—beyond a miracle, that is—of getting better. Children with all kinds of mental disabilities. Children in wheelchairs with no hope of walking. And I want you to witness the joy in their lives."

She opened her mouth as if to speak, then closed it and sank against the chair back.

"Please don't get angry at me, Emily. But these kids have no other hope than to live with their problems, yet they love and laugh. They strive to do the best with what they have."

"And I don't." She dropped her gaze to the table, dragging her fingers over the white-on-white design in the cloth.

"If you want me to make this easy for you to hear, I can't. Yes. You have every potential to walk again, yet you choose to sit in this chair without hope."

The air hung heavy with silence. Greg had so much more to say. For one, he'd mentioned two reasons. He hoped she didn't remember that.

"I'm not brave, Greg. I'm not courageous like those kids I saw this afternoon. It's plain old fear. I'm afraid."

"Afraid of what? That the surgery will fail? That you'll have pain? Because you will. Pain and frustration at trying to strengthen those underused muscles and tendons. I see that every day on the job. Is that what you fear?"

"That and…I don't know. It's something inside me."

She looked like a frightened child and he longed to hold her in his arms. "I'd like you to have a second opinion, Emily. Maybe another surgeon has a different solution for you, but I long to see you walk again…not for me but for you."

"I know you do, but I don't need a second opinion. This was the second opinion. I just don't understand why you care."

"It's the same reason I'd like you involved with me in Special Olympics." His heart thundered as his second reason pushed its way into his throat. He saw the red warning light of his emotions, but he edged forward.

"What is it?"

"I care about you."

"I know, Greg. You're a kind man. I see—"

He raised his moist palm and captured her fingers against the table. "No, Emily, I care for you differently than I care for the kids."

Her eyes widened, and she drew her hand away and clutched her chest. "It's only your compassion. I don't think that you should…" A deep gasp shuddered in her chest and covered her mouth.

"I shouldn't have told you here, Emily. I understand that you're still dealing with your husband's death. The whole tragedy—"

"Greg." She captured his attention with her direct gaze.

He faltered, letting the unspoken words slide back into his thoughts.

She studied him, her emotions a kaleidoscope. "I can't forget Ted's death, but I've dealt with it. What bothers me is my own life. My own lack of enthusiasm and courage. My own lack of faith."

"That's something you can fix."

"I can't fix it all. I'm not a whole person and—"

"Not whole?" Her words tore through him. "I never want to hear you say that."

She gaped at him wide-eyed.

"Are those kids you saw today not complete?" he said. "Are they less than human beings?"

"N-no...I didn't mean it that way."

"They're total kids. Whole and complete." He captured her fingers in his. "And so are you, Emily." Startled by his own emotion, Greg fought to keep his thoughts collected.

"You don't understand, but if it will make you happy, I'll volunteer to help the Special Olympics. I'll enjoy it...and I'm thinking about the surgery, Greg. Thinking and praying."

Startled by his reaction, Greg swallowed his emotion and managed a smile. "Praying is good, Emily." He wanted to tell her he'd been praying since he'd met her, but he decided to leave well enough alone.

Emily sealed the last envelope and placed it in the cardboard box. Handling a Special Olympics mailing was well within her ability. She slid the package to the back of the table and hoisted herself up from the chair.

Days had passed since their dinner and the emotion that charged through her, and Greg's words still rang in her ears. *Whole and complete.* The thought stung her heart. How could she tell him the truth?

He'd called daily and stopped by during the week to

drop off the envelopes. He'd even spent an hour spading some of the flower beds in her garden.

But tonight was different. Greg would be there for the evening to work on the planting. In preparation, Emily had purchased a few flats of annuals with Marti's help. She picked up bags of peat moss and composite, too, and then threw in a box of bone meal.

Each time they'd been together, her heart grew closer to him. She hummed, warmed by their growing friendship. If nothing more, his company meant everything to her.

She heard a car door slam and inched toward the back screen. Greg waved and opened the hatch to his cargo area, bringing out a cluster of gardening tools. He lay them on the grass, then headed up the porch steps.

"You didn't need to bring your tool shed. I have all that in the garage."

He opened the back door and stepped inside, then slid his arm around her shoulder. "But not my favorite trowel."

Standing beside him as she so rarely did, she admired his height inches above her head. The heat from his body and the pressure of his muscular arm around her shoulder made her feel cared for and protected.

He stretched his large hands in front of her. "And I bet you don't have garden gloves to fit these beauties."

His smile sent warm tendrils through her. "I doubt if mine would fit." She shifted her walker toward the door. "I'd like to come out and watch."

"Watch! No way. You'll help. You have two perfectly good hands. I've got the knees."

The *knees* reference dampened her pleasant thoughts. "Bad choice of word," she said.

"Sorry. I'll be more selective next time." His eyes shone with apology.

"I suppose this conversation isn't doing a thing for your

flower beds.'' He patted the chair and she settled onto the seat. Then he grasped the handles, pushed open the door with his back and wheeled her onto the porch, then down the ramp.

The scent of sunshine and earth wrapped around Emily as he wheeled her into the garden. When he stepped around to face her, a new aroma nuzzled her awareness—orange and spice, masculine and fresh.

''Why don't you have a woman in your life, Greg?'' The question slid from her lips as easy as a heel in mud. Too late to catch herself.

He looked at her with surprise. Yet beneath his expression, she saw something deeper. ''My work...and so many things. I dated in college. Not much since then.''

''You'd be a wonderful catch, you know. Besides handsome, you're the kindest man I know.'' She'd opened her mouth and decided to put her whole foot it in—muddy heel or not.

''I know. I have women dropping at my feet—''

''Maybe it's only their bad knees.'' She surprised herself.

He faltered, then his face broke into a big smile. ''I'd hoped it was my charm.''

''I didn't mean to ruin your dream.''

He ran his fingers across her cheek. ''You'll never ruin my dreams. You can only make them beautiful.''

Her heart lurched at the tone of his voice. Amazed, at his look and the tenderness in his voice, she scuffled to speak, wanting words to cover her emotions. ''I bet you say that to all the girls.''

''Only the ones I care about.''

The ones I care about. The thought filled her as sweetly as custard in a cream puff. His words swelled in her heart and aroused her imagination.

* * *

In the high school's wide hallway, Emily watched families stand in line, waiting to sign in for the Special Olympics competition. The large entrance buzzed with excitement.

Emily checked off names, smiling at eager-faced children and proud parents, then handed them programs. The experience warmed her as she greeted families she'd gotten to know from earlier practice sessions, and she was pleased she'd agreed to help.

When she finished the first round of registration, her replacement arrived and to her delight, Greg appeared beside her.

"Time for your break," he said, grasping the handles of her chair. "Let's watch some of the events."

"I'd love to." Images of familiar children marched through her mind.

Greg pushed her chair down the hallway. "How about some sunshine? We can watch the track competition."

Though sunshine tempted her, Butch's face settled in her thoughts. "Let's take a peek at the basketball event first. Do you mind?"

"Not at all…and I'm guessing you want to watch Butch," he said, guiding her wheelchair to a convenient space inside the gymnasium, then sliding onto the wooden bench.

"Thanks," Emily said, touched again by his thoughtfulness.

Amazed at the large, exuberant crowd that filled the bleachers, Emily listened to their encouraging cheers, but she watched in silence until Butch's eager movements caught her attention. Her heart melted as she thought of his upturned face and his words *He needs me.*

"Block him, Butch," she yelled. "That's it."

The crowd cheered as the ball bounced out of bounds.

Greg's chuckle reached her ear, and she turned to him seeing the knowing smile on his face.

"I see what you mean," she said.

He raised a brow as if he didn't understand.

"I see what you mean about me," she said. "The kids are brave and having fun whether they win or lose."

Greg's gaze locked with hers. "It's that old saying— it's how you play the game that's important."

Shame slithered through her, recalling her lack of faith. No trust in her surgeon or in God. She approached the surgery as if it were the guillotine, rather than a miracle offering her a chance to walk and live.

When had her faith vanished? She knew in part. She begged God for Ted's life, but God hadn't heard her. She altered her perspective. The Father heard everything. He'd answered no. But why?

That was the question that haunted her. Why had her loving husband died? And why did God allow her to walk after therapy, only to send her back to the wheelchair?

"Thinking?" Greg asked, his eyes questioning.

She nodded.

He tucked his hands into his trouser pockets and didn't pry.

But Emily wished he had. She needed to face her frustration and deal with her questions directly. "Ready?" she asked.

"Ready if you are," he said and guided the wheelchair out of the gymnasium.

The door leading to the outside stadium was nearby, and in a few moments, Emily filled her lungs with the warm spring air. She'd spent far too long inside her house with no sunshine to soothe her body or her heart. Her home had become a safe haven away from the world.

Greg took broad steps behind her, and they arrived at the stadium. The crowded area hummed with activity. Unable to use the bleachers with her chair, Greg found a spot along the front in the middle of the action. A young girl, waiting for her turn to participate, stood nearby, gazing at Emily. The child grinned and Emily returned her smile.

"Are you in the race today?" Emily asked.

The girl's head bobbed as she sidled closer. She pointed her finger at the chair. "Are you in the race, too?" She giggled as she ran her hand along the wheel.

"No, I'm just watching."

"You are?" The child's eyes widened. "But you're in a wheelchair." She popped her index finger into her mouth.

Emily chest tightened, hearing the girl's honesty. "I can't walk."

"Your legs don't work?"

Emily's heart ached as the child struggled to grasp her words. "My legs work, but they hurt."

"Oh." Sadness filled the child's face. "You can get them fixed."

Her candid truth struck Emily and she swallowed. Even a challenged child had the good sense to know that Emily's legs could be fixed. She glanced toward Greg, wondering if he heard. He appeared to be watching their interaction, but he didn't comment. Emily refocused on the child and returned the honesty. "I could, but I'm scared."

"Don't be scared. Jesus will take care of you." The child patted her arm.

Emily's eyes filled with tears, her voice only a whisper. "Yes, He will. Thank you." She brushed the moisture from her lashes. "What's your name?"

"Jenny. What's yours?"

"Emily. Are you going to run soon?"

"My mom said ten minutes." She held up both hands, her fingers spread wide in front of her. "Is it ten yet?"

"I don't know, but when you're in the race, I'll cheer for you, and maybe you'll hear me."

"Maybe." She nodded. "And if I don't win, don't be sad, 'cuz it's okay." She placed her hand on Emily's.

The child's touch worked its way around Emily's heart. "It doesn't matter if you don't win?"

"Nope. 'Cuz I'll be brave."

Before Emily could drag a response from her knotted throat, a woman beckoned to Jenny. The child waved goodbye and hurried away.

"Wisdom from babes," Greg said.

"I know, except I feel like the infant."

Her mind weighted with thoughts, Emily watched the children gather at the starting line, Jenny among them. Number fifteen. When the race began, the girl shot from the starting line and darted ahead of the others.

"Run, Jenny. Run," Emily called, but she knew Jenny didn't care at all. Win or lose, she'd run the race.

The first child crossed the finish line, but Jenny had fallen behind. Yet when she'd finished the race, her face glowed with the competition.

With a tearful grin, Emily looked at Greg. "She's a winner."

Greg ran his hand across her shoulders, then leaned over and kissed her hair.

Emily's heart lurched at his touch, and she grappled for a response. While she sat in silence a boy darted from the crowd and headed for Greg, saving her with the distraction.

"Robbie, you're looking good," Greg said to the child. "Are you running today?"

The boy chattered about the race and his surgery while Emily digested what Greg had done.

He'd kissed her hair.

Her mind whirred with questions. Who was Greg? A neighbor? A friend? Or was he more than a friend? Could their relationship be growing into love? Maybe a love that led to a lifetime commitment? Another chance to love and have a...

No. Not her. Sorrow knifed her thoughts and crushed her hope. Greg deserved a whole wife, one who could give him children—a family. She was not that woman.

When the boy left, Greg remained quiet, focusing on the racers. Emily did the same. Though she was silent, her mind was not. It continued its thoughtful monologue about the outcome of all that was happening in her life. One brave realization stuck out from the rest. Though marriage seemed impossible, the chance to walk did not.

When the race ended, Greg turned to her. "Are you ready to get back?"

"Sure," she said while thoughts spilled from her, crying to be spoken.

Greg steered her toward the building, but when they neared a bench shaded by a large elm, she raised her hand. "Do we have time to talk?"

"Time to talk?" Greg glanced at his watch, then eyed the bench. "Sure, all the time in the world."

Though he wore a concerned expression, he released the handles of her chair and sat near Emily. "You got so quiet back there, I figured something was wrong. Was it something I did?"

She could still feel the brush of his lips against her hair. How could she be angry at that? "Not really. It's me. I'm thinking about so many things. The little girl—Jenny— made me think about my lack of courage, again. I despise being so weak. It's a character flaw."

"We're all weak and flawed." He ran his hand down her arm while his eyes seemed weighted with sadness.

She studied his sorrow-filled eyes longing to know what troubled him. "It's my lack of faith...and anger," she said. "Anger for everything that happened these past years."

He slid his hand up her arm to her shoulder and gave it a gentle squeeze. "You've been through a lot, Emily."

"I know, but I don't like it. I keep asking myself why

God took Ted's life and resigned me to a wheelchair. I wish I'd just accept it and not feel so victimized.''

"Those things aren't easy to understand. The best we can do is have faith. Faith that in spite of our anxiety, doubt and skepticism, God is with us, willing to carry our burdens.''

"That's where I fail. I can't seem to let go of them. I want to lug them along with me.''

Greg captured her fingers and entwined them in his. "We're all like that, Emily. I sound so sure when I talk, but do you think I've let go of my pain and regret and walked away?'' He cocked his head. "Not by a long shot. I'm as flawed as you.''

Again he roused her curiosity. Why did he feel pain and what did he regret? She studied him for a moment. "Then what do we do?''

"You know as well as I do. We pray. Ask for strength and forgiveness…and faith.''

Forgiveness? Emily understood his need for strength and faith. By why forgiveness?

He brushed her cheek. "With faith, we can move mountains,'' he said.

"I'd just like to move my legs without pain.'' She chuckled, hoping to lighten the mood.

But Greg didn't laugh. He gave her a tender smile. "You have the solution for that already. You just have to act on it and have faith that God will take care of you.''

The gentle look sent her heart fluttering, and her thoughts easily to his gentle kiss—so simple. Yet the memory nudged her with apprehension.

Greg's tender attention gave her hope—hope she never considered having again, and she feared it.

Why? Because she didn't want to face the outcome. Embracing hope left her vulnerable. And she couldn't handle one more disappointment in her life. Ted's death, her crushed legs and damaged reproductive system had topped the atrocity charts.

Chapter Five

Emily's wheelchair thumped as Greg tossed it into the back of his SUV. He'd been both surprised and pleased when Emily asked him to drive her to a doctor's appointment. She'd seemed uneasy since the Olympics when he'd brushed her hair with a kiss. He hadn't meant to. It just seemed right and natural, but afterward, he'd wished he hadn't. She'd become tense and withdrawn.

His feelings for her had grown far more than he'd ever thought possible. In only a few weeks, he'd gone beyond being neighborly and kind, to enjoying her company, to wanting her in his arms.

Greg slammed the lid, rounded the vehicle and slid into the driver's seat. He would have to be honest with Emily soon before he acted again without thinking. Her friendship meant everything to him to destroy it…because he cared too much.

"Thanks for driving me to this appointment," Emily said. "Marti's tied up with wedding plans and—"

"No problem. I'm pleased you asked me."

"Pleased?" Her forehead wrinkled with confusion.

"I enjoy your company, Emily. I assume you know that."

A faint tinge of color brightened her cheeks. "You're a good man, Greg."

"I'm more than that. I'm…" He caught himself. "I'm your gardener. And speaking of him, he's doing a pretty good job with your flower beds. I checked them out before I knocked on the door."

Her flush cooled to a glow. "It does look nice."

Unexpectedly, she evaded his eyes and looked out the passenger window. "You've been a real gift to me. Not only the flowers, but my life. It felt empty for so long with no purpose, no direction. And now…I look forward to waking up each morning."

"I'm happy to hear that, Emily." He lowered his hand from the steering wheel and pressed it against hers resting on the seat between them. Though he longed to keep his palm pressed against her soft, cool skin, he withdrew it.

With both hands clasping the steering wheel, he searched for a safer topic.

Silence hummed in his ears.

"You mentioned Marti's being tied up with the wedding plans. How are things going?" he asked finally.

"Good," Emily said, turning her gaze from the window and shifting to face him. "She's holding the reception at the Venetian Club. It's a sit-down, family-style dinner. Not much more expensive than the buffet." A grin spread across her face. "I detest buffets."

"Me, too," Greg said.

"Really?"

"Really. Why are you surprised?"

"I hate them because they're awkward for me in this chair, but I thought men would feel differently."

"Not this man. I hate waiting in line and then choosing the wrong things."

She agreed as silence settled over her again.

He watched her smile fade.

"We looked for dresses last weekend." She rubbed the back of her neck, her features tensing. "I told you I'm Marti's matron of honor." Her sad gaze met his.

"I remember. Did you find dresses you like?" He knew her discomfort rose from something more serious than a dress style.

She blinked and lowered her head. "I can't convince Marti that she should replace me. She could ask one of her friends…or our cousin to do the honors." She lifted her gaze. "She doesn't listen."

"Good for her."

Her eyes widened with a look of surprised confusion.

"What's the problem?" He asked the question knowing the answer.

"A million things. The wheelchair. The photographs. Everything."

"You have time. Right? December?"

She nodded. "Just before Christmas." Her expression brightened for a moment. "Our gowns are green, and she's ordering red flowers. We'll look like Christmas trees."

Her unexpected humor caught Greg by surprise. His sudden laughter encouraged hers.

"Sounds perfect to me," he said. But his thoughts had turned away from the lighthearted image to one more serious.

"Do you really think so?" she asked. "Green and red. I don't know. And then me…in a wheelchair."

Greg took a chance. "If you agreed to the surgery soon, you'll be skipping down the aisle at the wedding."

Emily's heart whacked against her breastbone before skipping a beat. She lifted her hand and counted on her fingers. "Six months? Less than that. I doubt it."

"I'm a physical therapist. Trust me. You can be walking easily in six months."

The vision filled her mind. She pictured the long church aisle and imagined herself traipsing its length.

Despite her earlier sarcasm about color, Emily envisioned the lovely dresses—forest-green for her and a softer shade for the other female attendants. Perfect choices for the holiday. In her hands, she could imagine red and white roses mingled with baby's breath and tied with a red satin ribbon. Different and appropriate.

She pushed the vision aside and brushed tears from her eyes. Self-pity. She despised the feeling and pressed her lips together to keep from saying anything to Greg. He had too much faith, and she wasn't going to change his optimism.

Focusing on the landscape, Emily saw the office building appear on the right. She pointed, and Greg pulled into the lot to park.

Once settled into the wheelchair, Emily tensed as Greg pushed her into the waiting room. How many visits had it been? Too many without making a decision.

Today she had made up her mind.

Emily had been quiet since she'd left the surgeon's office. Greg wanted to pry, but he'd finally understood her way and knew he'd better let Emily tell him in her own good time what had happened.

When Greg pulled into her driveway, Marti's car wasn't there, and relief chased away his question. He wanted to talk to Emily in private. He climbed from the SUV, retrieved her chair and helped her shift from the car to the seat.

"Let's go out back," he said, not waiting for her answer.

As he rounded the corner, his pulse quickened seeing

the bright flowers rising above the well-pruned shrubs. Steering the chair forward, he noticed butterflies fluttering among the blossoms like petals playing on the wind.

"Look. You're surrounded by friends." He included himself in that category, but sometimes he wondered if Emily did.

He settled her chair near the bench and sat beside her, waiting and praying for her to tell him what had happened in the surgeon's office. Greg pulled his attention back to the butterflies, admiring their delicate beauty and fragile existence—so like Emily.

"I agreed to go ahead with the surgery." Her voice sounded as soft as the breeze.

His chest tightened as her words registered. "You did?" He leaned closer and slid his hand along Emily's arm, and though she tensed at his touch, she didn't pull away. Encouraged by his thankfulness, he eased her chin toward him. "Emily, I can't tell you how relieved I am. I'm not happy about the surgery, but I am about the prognosis."

Her eyes sought his, and he drew his hand along the line of her jaw to her lips, caressing them with his finger. Then drawing from his resolve, he rose from the bench and lowered his mouth to hers. A gentle, brief kiss and no more.

Tears filled her eyes, and he brushed them away. Though aching for her predicament, his heart surged with pleasure. She accepted his kiss, leaning into it, as fleeting as it was. "Don't cry, Emily. Everything will be wonderful."

"Self-pity," she said. "I'm a bundle of self-pity."

"No. You're not," he said, urging her from the chair so he could hold her in his arms.

She rested her weight against him. "I want to know I'm doing the right thing. I want to trust the surgeon."

"It's not the surgeon you need to trust, Emily. It's God. He's with you just like Marti and I will be."

She buried her face in his chest. "I'm so scared, Greg. I agreed to go through with it, but I'm frightened."

"It's not easy, I know, but it'll be wonderful when it's all over." He guided her attention to the garden. "Look at the butterflies. As pretty as you. And after the surgery, you'll be free of that chair and flitting through the garden like they are."

"That's what I keep telling myself." She drew back and inhaled. She shuddered.

Greg nestled her to his side, feeling her dainty body against his, as natural and amazing as the pattern left behind from the dust of butterfly wings.

When she'd calmed, Greg helped her to her chair. Today seemed the perfect time to give her the gift he'd purchased for her. "You wait right here," he said, backing away. "I have something for you."

Watching over her shoulder, Emily's pulse skipped a beat as Greg darted away. "What's the surprise?" she called after him. "Is it crutches?"

His laugh drifted to her.

"Or a nice walker?"

Greg vanished around the side of the house, probably missing her final comment. She caved back against the chair...a chair she might never use again after her surgery. The thought rose to heaven as a prayer.

Everyone wanted this for her. Everyone but her. She'd struggled with her thinking for so long, trying to understand. If she could walk, then why would she be lonely? Naturally, Marti would be gone—married and settled in her own home.

Her focus shifted to the garden. Butterflies of all sizes and colors—white ones, beige with whorls of brown and amazing orange monarchs. They hovered above the flowers, settled on a petal, then flitted away. So fragile and free from the cocoon that bound them.

Free from the cocoon. As much as she would miss Marti, a sweet reality washed over Emily. She could build a life again after her surgery. Return to the work she loved. Enjoy her garden.

She would…feel alive. Feel beautiful. Feel liberated.

"I hope you like this."

Greg's voice pulled her from her reverie. He stood beside her, holding a long wooden structure that resembled a three-foot birdhouse. But when he held it toward her, the house had no doors. Only long slits in its face.

"It looks like a birdhouse for skinny sparrows. What is it?"

"A butterfly house."

She eyed the narrow cuts in the natural wood covered by a slanted roof. "I've never heard of such a thing." She analyzed his expression to see if he were teasing.

He propped the wooden structure on his hip. "The woman who loves butterflies. The woman who lures them to her garden with flowers. And she's never heard of a butterfly house?" He shook his head, his face brightened by a teasing grin.

"So I don't know everything," she goaded, enjoying the lighthearted moment that helped to ease her doubts. "What's it for?"

"Protection. It gives those fragile creatures a safe haven. A shelter to protect them from bad weather or critters that might harm them."

He astounded her. She'd never considered owning a house for butterflies. A place to feel safe.

In her peripheral vision, her own house came into focus. Her private safe haven. But butterflies left their shelter and enjoyed the sunshine. For so long, she hadn't.

"Thank you," she said. "I love it. It's perfect."

"And so are you," he said.

She shook her head. "I'm not perfect." Riddled with doubts and raw fears, she felt far from perfect.

His expression grew tender. "I can have my own opinion."

"I suppose you can." He made her grin. "Then I should say thanks."

He brushed his fingers against her cheek. "I'll put this up once we decide on a good place. On the elm tree near the lilacs might be a good spot." He lay the gift on the end of the bench.

"I think so." She reached out and grasped his hand. "Help me up. I want to hug you for the present."

He stepped closer and supported her as she rose.

Emily narrowed the space between them, her heart tripping over itself as she wrapped her arms around his waist and squeezed. "Thank you for the lovely surprise. It's so special."

He tilted her chin upward and gazed into her eyes. "Emily, you are special. Perfect and special."

His words fluttered through her like a million butterflies. She sensed something in the air—something fresh and exciting. She saw his lips nearing hers and held her breath.

Without hesitation, his mouth pressed against hers. She faltered, the feeling so alien, so exciting. But the tender touch roused her sleeping senses, and she lifted herself, yielding to his gentle caress, mouths locked in unspoken promises.

When she felt ready to burst, he drew back, his gaze locked to hers, and a sigh shuddered through her. He nestled her closer in his arms, one hand at her waist, the other on the nape of her neck, gently caressing her hair. Gooseflesh rose on her arms.

"You're beautiful," Greg whispered. "Inside and out."

Her pulse escalated with his comment. Another thank-you seemed too empty. She wanted to offer him more, but what did she have? "It's been so long," she said, her voice sounding breathless in her ears.

"For me, too. I've been away from the dating scene for years." He tilted her chin upward and gazed in her eyes. "I care about you more than I've cared for any other woman."

She studied his face, praying that he meant every word. "You don't have to say that if you're only being kind. I'll get over this…after the surgery."

"I know you will." He sent her a smile to melt her heart. His gaze drifted toward the garden. "Let's find a place to put the butterfly house."

"I'd like that."

He nuzzled his cheek against her hair, then grasped the wooden structure from the bench and paused as if in thought. "Over there by the elms."

Emily nodded. "That'll work. It's close to a bed of butterfly weeds."

He grinned, retreating to the bench and placing the house beside Emily. "I suppose I might need a nail and hammer."

"It usually helps." His excitement filled her with happiness…like a child with a new toy.

He vanished behind her, but in a heartbeat reappeared. "I've been thinking. Before you go into the hospital, I thought I'd bring my mom over to see your garden. What do you say?"

"Could I make dinner for you?"

"Something simple, if you want," he said.

"Simple is all you get from me."

"Nothing about you is simple, Emily. Trust me."

Chapter Six

Greg opened the passenger door to help his mother exit.

"I hope you're a gentleman with all the ladies," she said with a grin. "I taught you right."

"That you did, Mom." He gave her shoulder a pat, then took her arm and guided her up the walk.

Greg rang the bell, and in a moment, Emily greeted them and inched aside to give them entrance. "Welcome. Glad you could come." She gave Greg a teasing glance. "And you, too."

He chuckled and squeezed her arm, wanting so badly to kiss her flushed checks. He could tell she was flustered, trying to prepare the dinner. Her short copper-toned hair framed her usual translucent skin. Today it was a warm pink.

"We finally meet," the woman said. "I'm Rose, Greg's mother."

"Emily Casale, and I'm so happy to meet you, too."

"Greg told me about your lovely garden."

"It's only lovely because of Greg." Emily touched his

arm and gave it a squeeze. "And thanks so much for the tubers. They're in bloom and beautiful."

"Greg knows his way around a trowel," Rose said.

Greg shushed her. "Don't give away all my secrets."

Emily's face brightened with their banter. "Please—" she gestured through the archway "—let's sit in the living room. I didn't mean to keep you planted next to the front door."

Thank-yous and chuckles blended as they made their way into the living room.

"Your home is lovely, dear," Rose said, settling into a floral print easy chair. "Everything is so cozy."

"Thanks." She turned her attention to Greg. "Would you mind carrying in some iced tea or lemonade while I check on dinner."

"We could look at the garden while you finish," Greg said. "Unless you prefer to join us."

"No. Go head. Use the back door. It's closer."

He figured being out of her way was a good idea. They followed her into the kitchen, wrapped in the scent of herbs and chicken.

"Something smells wonderful," Rose said. "And what a pretty kitchen."

"Thanks." Emily motioned to the oven. "I made chicken divine. I hope you like it."

"We'll like anything you make, Em."

She did a double take hearing the nickname. "I haven't been called that since my mother died."

"It's a nice name," Rose said. She walked to the window beside the table and gazed outside. "Such a lovely view from here. I'm sure you could sit right here and look at the view all day long."

"I've been known to do that...in my more depressed moments."

Though she grinned, Greg suspected there had been more truth than humor in her comment.

"Let's take a look and let Emily finish dinner," he said to Rose.

His mother agreed and followed Greg through the back door. He took her arm and helped her down the steps.

When they stood at the edge of the garden, Rose spread out her arms at her sides and drew in a lengthy breath. "Smell the fragrance, Greg? Emily put a great deal of effort and love into designing this garden. It'll be wonderful when she can enjoy it again."

Agreeing, he breathed in the scented air while the weight of his mother's words pressed against his heart. "I don't understand how she sat here day after day and didn't fight to walk. When I first met Emily, she broke my heart."

They wandered along the path, Rose pausing occasionally to admire a flower, then ambling on again.

Rose paused in the center of the garden and eyed Greg. "You've fallen in love. It's obvious and so nice."

He laughed and wrapped his arm around her shoulders. "Thanks for telling me, Mom."

"It's nothing to be ashamed of. Love finds us wherever we are…even if we're hiding," she said. "I'm not sure why you've fought loving someone for so long." She patted his arm. "But God guides our stubborn steps and gets us to the right place eventually…when we stop struggling."

"I haven't been avoiding romance. I've just been busy helping people get well." He gave her a lopsided grin. "And even spent a little time with my mother."

"That's a job, Greg…not a life."

Her wisdom nailed him to the grass.

She patted his arm and pushed him along the path. "But things are different now. I'm so glad you found this woman. She's lovely and a good person. All she needs is a little nudge of confidence to get on with her life.''

''And you have a plan, I suppose?'' Greg knew his mother.

''It's God's plan.'' She faced him and reached up to put her hands on his shoulders. ''I'm just the instrument to help it along.''

His mother's sly smile made him chuckle.

Before they ambled back to the house, Rose stopped to inspect the dahlias. ''They look good.'' She lifted her sparkling gaze to his. ''I guess you did learn something from your mom.''

''I learned lots from her. Didn't have much choice.''

''You!'' she said, giving him a playful swat. ''I was too good to you.''

Their laughter greeted Emily's ears as she opened the back door. Their family love filled her and squeezed at her heart. What would she do if Greg walked away? He'd awakened her spirit, but he'd also made her vulnerable— a feeling she feared.

''Just in time,'' Emily said, motioning them to the table by the window.

''Smells great,'' Greg said, shyly nestling his arm around Emily's waist.

Heat rose to her cheeks. She knew it wasn't the oven, and so did Rose, evidenced by her smiling eyes.

''The flowers are beautiful, Emily. I couldn't believe the number of butterflies. You do have a way with them.''

''Thanks. It's a butterfly garden,'' Emily said. ''Many of the flowers attract butterflies.''

''Sounds lovely, and I'm sure that's not the only thing in your garden that's alluring.'' Rose gave Greg a knowing look.

''Mom has a sense of humor,'' Greg said, arching an eyebrow toward his mother.

"Thank you, dear," Rose said, looking as guilty as a jaywalker.

"Anyway, it's the flowers." She swallowed her embarrassment. "Not me."

His mother chuckled and changed the subject. "I think I'll buy one of those garden benches. Such a nice place to sit among the blossoms and watch the birds."

Emily couldn't help but grin at the wiry woman. "Greg brought just about everything back to life."

Everything back to life. Even her, in so many ways.

"Some things take longer to rejuvenate than others," Rose said. "But with a little nurturing…and prayer, all things work together for good who love the Lord."

A fitful silence settled over the room, and Emily wondered if Rose were talking about something other than flowers.

Greg cleared his throat, breaking the quiet.

Drawing herself from her muddled thoughts, Emily motioned again to the table. "Please. Find a seat."

Greg held a chair for his mother, and when she was seated, Emily handed him the chicken casserole and the garden salad. When the dinner rolls were on, Greg took his place, and Emily lowered herself into the chair with a confined grimace and slid the walker against the wall.

They had waited for her with folded hands. Emily bowed her head and asked a blessing on the food and her company. "Help yourselves," she said, passing the salad.

They filled their plates, murmuring an occasional comment while concentrating on their food. Emily sidled a look at Greg and his mother, realizing how lonely her life had been. The kitchen chair where Emily sat had become her place of solace. The landscape and birds brought evidence of the changing seasons, life moving past her window.

Moving past. That's what she'd done for so long—let

life pass her by. God willing, she would walk again—not run perhaps, but she'd keep up with life.

"I imagine you'll be happy to get this surgery over with," Rose said, as if she'd read her mind. "It takes courage."

"That or stupidity." Emily grinned, but fear churned in her stomach.

"Wisdom," Rose said. "You'll be walking before you know it. Greg can vouch for that." She motioned toward him with her fork. "And you know I'll keep you in my prayers, dear." Compassion etched Rose's voice.

"Thank you." Emily had been caught off guard by her kindness.

"And let Greg know if you need me after surgery," Rose added. "I'll be here for you."

Shame scooted up Emily's spine. Rose had offered her prayers and her help while Emily had done so little for herself. She'd left God right out of her dilemma. She'd always believed...but she hadn't trusted.

"Are you all right?" Greg asked.

She jerked her head upward. "Yes. I'm fine." She turned to Rose. "I was thinking how I'm always trying to stand on my own feet...and with bad knees at that."

Her words brought a smile to their faces...and to her own. She needed to smile. She needed Greg and his mother.

And she needed God.

The light blurred above Emily's head as she lay on the table in preop, waiting for the orderlies to wheel her away. Warmth rose up her arm where the needle sent a calming liquid to her consciousness.

"Getting sleepy?" Marti asked, seated at her side.

"Mmm-hmm," she said, trying to stay in focus. "What

time is it?'' Emily's mouth felt drier than sand, and she struggled to push the words to her lips.

"Eight. They should be here in a few minutes. Then I'll see you in a few hours in your room." Marti's cool hand pressed her arm. "Now relax."

"How's the patient?"

With foggy eyes, Emily gazed at the parted curtain. Greg stood at the foot of the gurney, dressed in his hospital smock.

"Greg." Her eyes closed and she tugged them open.

He stepped to her side and covered her hand with his. "How are you doing, Em?"

"Okay." Her voice sounded thick in her ears.

"Did Pastor Ben drop by?" he asked.

"Just for a few minutes," Marti answered. "He said a wonderful prayer and told us he'd come back in a couple of days."

"Good." Greg leaned down and pressed his warm lips to her icy cheek.

"I'm so cold. Am I...dying?" Emily asked.

Their snickers rang distantly in her ears. Greg squeezed her hand. "You're drifting into twilight, just like I told you. Let yourself go, and the next time you open your eyes it'll be over."

"Do like he says." Marti's faraway voice echoed into Emily's fading thoughts.

Greg took a last look at Emily's sleeping form and left the preop room, his mind a jumble. Who would have thought his feelings would have grown so deeply for Emily in the short time they'd known each other? But they had.

"Time for coffee?" Marti asked.

He checked his wristwatch. "Sure. I have about twenty minutes before I have to be back on the floor. We've been a little slow today."

She nodded, and they walked in silence to the elevator, then to the first floor. In the Mackenzie Cafeteria, Greg insisted on buying the coffee, and he added a couple of doughnuts to the tray. The large alcoves were near empty, and they found a quiet corner and sat.

"What do you really think?" Marti asked after a thoughtful length of silence.

Her surprise question yanked Greg from his own concerns. "She'll be fine, Marti. More than fine."

Tension slid from her face, and a grin appeared. "I should be ashamed, I suppose. Where's my faith now?" She lifted the cup and took a sip, but held it poised for a moment as if in thought before returning it to the table. "I worry so much about Emily. She frustrates me, but I love her dearly."

"She knows you've been concerned about the wedding. She wants—"

"That's part of it, I suppose." Her gaze drifted away for a moment before returning to him. "It's more than that."

More than that? Greg considered all the effects of Emily's disability on Marti's life. "It would be hard for her to be alone…without you at the house."

"True, but she's strong and I know she'll adjust."

Marti's words hung before him like a puzzle. Playing guessing games didn't sit well with Greg. What was the problem? What worried her?

Marti lifted the coffee to her lips, sipped and replaced the mug on the table. "Emily was a different person before the accident. Different in many ways."

More pieces of the puzzle. Greg watched tears rim Marti's eyes and glisten on her lashes.

"I want only the best for her," she said. "She's been through so much."

"She has," he said, feeling his own sorrow rising to the

surface. Greg thought of Emily's lost husband and her life in the wheelchair. "Once she's walking again I think her life will get back to normal." He lifted the cup and watched the coffee swirl around the rim before taking a sip.

"Normal?"

Cupping his mug in his hand, Greg peered at Marti. What could he say? Not normal with artificial knees perhaps, but leading a fulfilled life. A husband and family. That's what he meant. The vision pressed against his heart. Despite his conviction to remain single, Greg knew he wanted to be that man.

He loved children, and though he'd struggled for years over Aaron's death, he knew the time had come to deal with it, then move on with his life. A life with children. Lots of children.

Calming his thoughts, Greg lowered his coffee. "By normal, I meant…getting married again. Having a family."

"Probably not," she said, her eyes focused through the window.

When she turned back, Greg saw sadness in them.

"She may marry," Marti said, "but she may never have children."

"Never…have children?" The news hit him like a punch in the solar plexus. He thought about Emily with the kids at Special Olympics. The way her eyes sparkled when she talked with them. The joy that brightened her face. He couldn't imagine Emily never having children.

"The accident, Greg. Doctors warned her she'll probably never have a child." She lifted the coffee cup to her lips and poised there as if waiting for his response.

Unable to speak, Greg only stared at her.

Chapter Seven

On the way back to her room following therapy, Emily's legs throbbed, and today she missed Greg. He'd become so important to her, and the truth scared her.

Since the surgery he'd seemed different, and she wondered if his friendship had been motivated by her disability and not by his feelings for her. It was too late now. He'd already tied himself to her heartstrings, and she'd be lost without him.

Today Greg had a day off, and she had to deal with another therapist's treachery. Greg had become her favorite tormentor, forcing her to bend her leg to ninety degrees. A feat she'd once thought easy now seemed impossible. He insisted she lay on her back and lift her legs into the air, lowering them an inch a minute. And then she tackled stair climbing. Absurd, but she did it anyway.

The orderly scooted the wheelchair down the drab hallways while Emily clung to the chair arms, wondering if someone would step from a doorway and fall over her aching legs.

Her fourth day of therapy had come and gone, and if

the doctor agreed, she would go home tomorrow. She could hardly believe it. Still pessimistic thoughts bounced through her head, hard and reckless like a tennis ball.

How would she manage all day alone while Marti worked? And what about Greg? He'd told her he cared about her, but could she trust him? Would he vanish from her life once she could walk again?

Walk again? Would she ever really walk again? After four days, each step seemed a mile of pure torture.

Dashing through the doorway, Greg clutched his cumbersome package and looked at the empty bed. Therapy, he thought. Setting the gift on the hospital table, he felt pleased he'd used the ponderous time to buy her a surprise.

He needed something to fill his mind. Activities. Anything. Since Marti had told him about Emily's accident and the prognosis, his happiness had faded like sunshine behind storm clouds.

No children.

The sad image pressed against his heart. Sadness for Emily…and for himself.

Realizing he'd hidden his feelings from nobody but himself, Greg faced the truth. He loved Emily and wanted her to be his wife…to share his life and love…to bear his children. His chest tightened and sorrow formed in tears behind his eyes.

Glancing at the empty doorway, he pulled up a visitor's chair, but before he could settle down to wait, the bathroom door opened, surprising him.

Emily stood at the threshold, leaning against her walker. Her hair looked freshly combed while color rose on her cheeks.

"Greg."

He turned, opening his arms. "I missed you, Em. You

look wonderful." He leaned across the walker to brush a kiss on her cheek.

"I combed my hair. It's amazing what that can do."

"I figured you were at therapy, getting a workout."

"I just got back."

"How was it?" he asked.

"Terrible. I did the stairs today and all the leg lifts. I'm tired and miserable, and I just want to go home."

"You're depressed, Em. It's natural when you've had major surgery. It won't be long and you'll be home. Maybe tap dancing." He managed a lighthearted smile.

"Is tap dancing another form of torture?" She moved the walker toward him.

Greg backed away and let her maneuver toward the bed. Instead, she stopped at the armchair. "I think I'll try sitting a little."

"Do you have something to prop under your leg?"

"I'll be fine for a few minutes." She looked past him toward the hospital table. "What's that package?"

"A present." He grinned and handed her the long cylindrical object.

She eyed the gift and felt beneath the paper, giving him a knowing smile.

"You guessed," he moaned, sinking onto the bed's edge and pretending disappointment.

She tore off the wrapping and gazed at the hand-carved cane, running her fingers along the polished wood. "It's beautiful."

Greg had admired the cane more than any he'd seen. Winding from top to bottom, an intricate design of flowers and leaves had been worked into the deep-toned wood. "It's cherry. I've never seen anything like it."

"It's a work of art. Almost too lovely to use."

"But I expect you to use it…once you're strong enough.

When you don't need it anymore, you can prop it in your antique umbrella stand.''

"Thanks." She ran her finger over the elaborate design. "Here I figured I'd have to waddle around with one of these generic metal contraptions…with three prongs."

"You look more like a four-prong type to me."

Her face glowed with his teasing. He yearned to draw her against his chest and feel her heart beat in rhythm with his. More than anything, he longed to tell her that he knew the secret sorrow she kept inside, but he couldn't. He knew Emily too well. She had to be the one to open her heart.

"When will you go home?" he asked.

"Tomorrow, if the doctor signs the papers. I've already spoken to the home care rep. I'll have a visiting nurse and one of their physical thera—"

"And your own *private* therapist."

"I didn't know you made house calls."

Greg looked at the empty bed on the other side of the room and threw good sense to the sky. He rose, braced his hands on her chair arms and kissed her.

Drawing back, he gazed into her misty green eyes. Never in his career had he been attracted to even the most lovely patient, but today he had to admit, Emily was the woman he loved with all his heart.

Tears pooled in Emily's eyes as she sat in the recliner in her living room, her legs propped on the raised footrest. She's longed to return home and now that she was here, she was miserable. Lonely. Sad. Discouraged.

She eyed the bruise on her arm from the transfusion she'd received before convincing the surgeon to release her.

"Stop feeling sorry for yourself," Emily said aloud. She'd gotten her wish to come home. But for the past five days, she'd almost longed to be back in the hospital where people brought her meals, nurses came when she pushed the intercom, visitors arrived bearing flowers and life pulsated around her. Now, Marti was working, and Emily felt semistranded, a prisoner in her own home. No driving. No stairs without assistance. No Greg.

Greg had let her down. He'd called a couple of times and stopped by late one evening on his way home from a meeting, but that had been all. He'd promised to see her yesterday, but an emergency at the hospital caused him to work a double shift. Was this the beginning of what she'd feared?

Emily shook her head to dislodge her pity party. Her sister had done the best she could. Before Marti left for work, she'd fixed juice and cereal for Emily's breakfast. She'd had yogurt for lunch. Strawberry, not even a favorite flavor like key lime or raspberry. A little better than bread and water for the prisoner.

And now Marti had called to say she'd be late. Hearing her apologetic voice, Emily told her not to worry and that she could handle a can of soup for dinner. But no one understood how difficult it was to carry anything when both hands were grasping a walker. She hated struggling to stand on two alien knees. Knees that felt as if they belonged to someone else. She shook her head, tired of her whining.

The doorbell rang, and she hesitated. Tuesday. She wasn't expecting anyone. The visiting nurse had come in the morning, and her home care therapy wasn't due until Thursday.

With apprehension, she pushed her body from the chair, feeling helpless and vulnerable. When she pulled open the door, her pulse skittered.

"Greg. I wasn't expecting you." She shifted from his friendly face and focused on his arms, burdened with two large grocery bags.

"Can I come in?"

Realizing she and her walker blocked his entrance, she stepped aside. "Sure. Come in." She closed the door. "I'm just surprised. I wasn't expecting you."

"I know. I'm a little late." He grinned. "About twenty-four hours to be exact, but last night couldn't be helped. Those are situations we never count on."

He stepped to her side and gave her a perfunctory kiss. "Now, I want you to sit while I make dinner."

"You what?"

He nodded toward the two bags clutched in his arms. "You didn't think I brought my laundry, did you?"

Confused, she shook her head while her mind dwelled on the fleeting casual kiss.

He headed for the kitchen as she returned to the recliner. In a moment, Greg came back to the living room, his arms empty.

"In case you're wondering," he said, "I called Marti at her office to tell her about my idea to cook dinner. She said she had to work so it was a great plan."

"She knew you were coming?" Emily was surprised Marti hadn't hinted at least.

"I told her not to tell you." He hesitated, eyeing her position in the chair. "Why aren't you keeping your legs elevated?"

"I am, Mr. Therapist." She pulled the lever on the recliner and her feet rose.

"I think you need a pillow under them, too." He pulled a toss pillow from the sofa and slid it beneath her calves. "Let me have a look."

She rolled up her pant legs while he eyed the staples.

"Looks good. Do they hurt?"

"No. They feel wonderful. I hope to have staples in my legs forever."

"Good attitude," he said, ignoring her sarcasm. He

stepped back. "And now you can watch my transformation from therapist to chef." He winked and hurried from the room.

Emily listened to the cabinet doors slamming, the pans banging and dinnerware clinking. She'd expected Greg to call out a million questions, but he managed without asking one. Longing to watch, she harnessed her curiosity and remained with her legs on the pillow as Greg had ordered.

Finally, a savory aroma drifted into the living room. Her stomach rumbled as the tempting odor stirred her taste buds and aroused her appetite. When she thought she could wait no longer, Greg came through the doorway.

"Time to eat," he said, crossing to her chair to help her rise.

Using the walker, Emily made her way into the kitchen. When she reached the doorway, she eyed the table set with place mats, china and in the center, a tossed salad. But before she could reach the kitchen chair, Greg had moved to her side.

"I've been longing to do this," he said, supporting her as he slid the walker to the side. He enveloped her in his arms and nestled her to his chest. "You don't know how I've yearned to hold you." His eyes sought hers and held them captive. "The hospital didn't seem the right spot for an employee to cuddle one of the patients."

"Probably not," she said, recalling how she longed to be in his arms despite her pain.

He tilted her chin upward, then drew his finger along her lower lip and caressed her cheek. His hand slid to the nape of her neck and rested in her hair as his mouth met hers.

Warmth radiated through her. Her loneliness and concern melted away as she nestled in his arms. When he drew back, his tender look sent a sigh fluttering through her chest.

"Is it warm in here?" he asked, his cheeks dimpling with his grin. "You'd better sit before the chef ruins his gourmet dinner."

An easy chuckle bubbled from Emily's throat. It felt good. Days had passed since she felt cheerful enough to laugh.

Greg helped her sit before taking the steaks from the broiler.

"I knew I smelled something wonderful." Emily eyed the thick, perfect filets.

He pulled two large potatoes from the microwave, split the tops and daubed them with butter. When he settled into the chair, he clasped her hand for the blessing.

Guilt rose in her again. All her plans to place her burdens on God fell by the wayside. Her commitment vanished from her thoughts.

Following the amen, Greg kept her fingers in his. "I've neglected you, Emily, and not by choice. So many things have gotten in my way."

His gentle expression enveloped her. "I've been feeling sorry for myself. It seems everyone wanted me to have this surgery, and now—"

"I know." He bent down and kissed her fingers. "I persisted and then like an uncaring soul, I let things get in my way. I vanished."

"You didn't vanish."

"No, but I've made cameo appearances. I hadn't meant for that to happen." He eyed the neglected steak and grasped his fork. "Enough excuses. Time to dig in before our food gets cold."

Hearing his apology, she relaxed and lifted the fork. His gentle manner made her comfortable. Yet against her will, nagging fears continued to dominate her thoughts. Once she had loved and lost. Could it happen again?

Stark reality smacked her. If Greg loved her, what did she have to offer? Only herself…and was that enough?

Ashamed of her continual worries, she pushed them into the far corner of her mind. Tonight Greg sat beside her, sharing a meal that he'd prepared. What more could any woman want?

She dished up the fresh garden salad, then sliced into the pink steak. Perfect.

Emily ate in silence, enjoying the meal and the quiet. Filled, she pushed back her plate. "I can't eat another bite."

"But I brought dessert."

"You thought of everything," she said.

"It's from the bakery. A peanut-butter cheesecake."

Her favorite. Greg's thoughtfulness overwhelmed her, and her receded tears found their way into her eyes. She blinked to push them back. "How about later?"

"Sounds good. We'll have it after a little P.T."

"P.T.?" Emily raised an eyebrow. She knew P.T. meant physical therapy, but she had no thought of it today. Thursday was her day.

"I've neglected you. Remember…I'm your personal therapist. You have to exercise everyday so why not—"

"Because I'd rather do it alone."

He shook his head. "I know. Then you can cheat and don't try as hard."

She jutted her chin upward in defiance. "I do, too, try."

"You look as guilty as sin." He gathered plates from the table and carried them to the sink. "You prop up your leg in the recliner, and I'll be there as soon as I clean the kitchen."

Realizing she'd never win the battle, Emily did as he asked, waiting for her handsome tormentor to ply his wiles on her legs.

When Greg returned to the living room, he brought

along a kitchen chair. "Let's start here." He patted the seat.

Emily released the recliner footrest and boosted herself from the seat and eased her way to the chair.

He stood back and watched. "Show me how far back you can push your leg."

She tried but as soon as the pain came, her will failed her.

Greg knelt down and added pressure.

"You can't make it go back any farther," Emily moaned as he forced her foot beneath the chair, coercing her knee to bend at a sharp angle.

"Sure, it does," he said with an understanding smile.

"But it hurts."

"Not you! It hurts me, Mr. Physical Therap—Tormentorist."

"You have a great sense of humor, Em." He chucked her under the chin.

"It's that or strangle you." She winced. "Or cry."

"Let's just stick with your wit and forget the threats. I'm too young to meet my Maker."

"Then keep that in mind the next time you contort my knees that much."

He rose and patted her arm. "But how else will you walk if we don't get these legs working like new?"

Her heart sank. "They are new. That's my problem."

He ignored her. "How about some leg lifts?" He pulled her walker in front of her chair.

Emily rose, relieved that he'd finished that part of her exercise. "I like you better as a friend. Do you know that?"

"I know…but it's because I care so much."

"You sound like my mother making me take awful-tasting medicine," Emily said.

"Just finish these lifts and it will hold you for today." He stood back and watched. "Push. Push."

She gave him an evil eye.

He ruffled her hair. "Walking is good. Go outside when someone's here to help you. Enjoy the end of summer."

"You expect me to traipse around the neighborhood clinging to this walker?"

"How about the driveway. You could put a bag over your head so no one recognizes you."

The image gave her a hearty laugh.

"Okay, then, we have that problem solved." He helped her back to the chair and plopped onto the sofa.

"I suppose I should say thank you," Emily said, shifting to relax her legs on the recliner footrest.

"You're welcome." He grinned.

"I've really missed you."

An unexpected look rose on his face. Discomfort? Apprehension?

Emily's breathing shallowed, wondering what it meant. She'd come to learn Greg couldn't hide his feelings. His face told it all. "What's wrong?"

He released an uneasy sigh. "I might as well get this over with."

Her stomach lurched, and she held her breath. Could her fears be coming true? He'd been scarce since her surgery and today's generosity could be just a kind way to say goodbye.

She forced the words from her throat, not wanting to hear the answer. "What is it? What's wrong?"

Chapter Eight

"I'll be gone again for a few days. On Thursday, I'm flying out to Denver for a training workshop. I won't be back until midweek. I'm filling in for another therapist."

Emily struggled to cover her disappointment. "You seem to do a lot of filling in."

"It's part of my job, Em. I'm sorry. The medical field changes daily. We're constantly being briefed on new procedures and equipment."

"I know. I'm just—"

"Disappointed. Be patient."

"Easy for you to say."

"It's not easy, Em."

But it was easy. Easier to be discontent than face life. Except for Marti, Emily had been alone a long time. Why was it different now? Why did she feel more lonely today than she did a few months ago? She knew the answer. Greg. Hopes and dreams. She had to stop and face reality before life crumbled in on her.

Greg took a deep breath. "I suppose I should go. I have

a busy day tomorrow.'' He gazed down at her legs. "When does the nurse visit again?''

"Friday morning. I'll be fine.''

"With all the prayers we've all sent up for you, you should be indestructible,'' Greg said, flashing her a warm smile.

A snide comment rolled across her tongue and she swallowed her words. He hadn't known her when she prayed over and over for Ted to live. If prayers had been all it took, Ted would be standing beside her now. If prayers were answered, she'd have her own knees. If prayers were answered…

Standing by the Arrivals/Departures monitor, Greg checked his departing flight. On time. He eyed his wristwatch. He had a few minutes before boarding, and as always, his thoughts turned to Emily. Concern jabbed at him. In the past weeks, he sensed something going on with her, something he couldn't decipher. He'd tried to put a name to it. Withdrawal. Apprehension. An emotion without a name. Nothing he could solve because he didn't understand the problem.

He'd grown to care for her…love her, if he were honest, but he'd been anxious since his talk with Marti, trying to imagine life without a child. His own child.

Though marriage had eluded him, stifled by his own preoccupation with his career, now that the possibility arose, marriage and family seemed to go together. He was certain many marriages were fulfilled without children, but…his joy in life had been working with kids. For him, marriage and children seemed inseparable.

Could loving Emily overcome his desire to be a father…to have a child of his own? He'd pondered and prayed. Adoption was possible. Would that be the answer? Would that fulfill his longing to be a parent?

Since Emily's surgery, he'd been neglectful. Had he used his job as an excuse? He didn't think so, but guilt poked at his reasoning. He'd hoped to remedy his distractions. Now this Denver trip threw his plan out of kilter again.

Greg hadn't meant to fall in love with Emily…or anyone. But despite his resolve, he sensed God leading him to her, and Emily had nestled in his heart as silently and tenderly as a butterfly on a blossom.

But how did Emily really feel about him? Their growing relationship had faltered…as if she were afraid to love. Recently he'd felt the wall rising between them. Slowly at first, but now the barrier seemed higher and stronger. Not that they didn't talk and laugh, but something blocked the warm honesty that they'd enjoyed.

Greg's heels clicked along the terminal's tile floor as if numbering the questions and thoughts that barraged his mind. Why did Emily fear loving him? He tried to put himself in her shoes. She'd lost a husband, and with that, she'd lost her trust in God. She'd lost hope.

His internal fear surfaced. Was it children? Did she refuse to love him because she couldn't have children? Greg had prayed about that, too. With God all things were possible…so what did he fear? He wanted Emily to have trust and faith. But where was his own?

The situation filled him with shame. How long would he harbor the guilt and anguish over his brother's death? He'd been only a child, and it had been an accident—but an accident based on carelessness. If he'd told Aaron no—not allowed him to ride the sled with him down the dangerous hill—Aaron would be alive today. He'd never told the truth to his parents, and he hadn't found courage to share that with Emily. If he weren't open with her, how could he expect her to be honest with him? If he hadn't forgiven himself, how could he expect Emily to forgive?

Greg stepped onto the moving sidewalk. In a minute, he'd be at his departure gate. He checked his watch. He still had time to call Emily. When his foot hit the solid floor again, he headed for the nearest telephone.

Punching in her number, Greg waited. When he heard her voice, his shoulders relaxed.

"Just checking in to see how you're doing."

"Greg."

Her halted response concerned him. "Are you okay?"

"I'm fine…but I thought you were leaving this morning."

"I'm at the airport."

"You're calling me from the airport? Is something wrong?"

"No. I was…thinking about you." He rethought his response. "No. About us, Em."

Silence.

"I wish I didn't have to go. I have so much I want to…" *Think about. I need to think. I can't hurt this woman. Dear Lord, give me direction here.*

"You have so much what?"

Her voice sounded frightened. Greg wanted to kick himself for making things worse rather than better. "I have so many things getting in my way, Em, but I'll be back in a few days and…"

"I'll be fine, Greg. Please don't worry. I have the visiting nurse and the therapist. And…I have Marti."

But do you have me, Em?

"Are you there?" Her sad voice echoed across the wire.

"I'm here, but I have to run. My plane is boarding. The sooner I get there, the sooner I'll be back."

"Have a safe trip."

"Thanks, Em. We have to talk when I get home. I'll see you then." *I love you,* he said to himself as he placed the receiver on the phone.

He needed to think and to explain his feelings. He needed most of all to understand the emotions and concerns that rattled in his head. Greg prayed the fortress he and Emily had built around themselves would crumble once he returned from Denver...and they had time to talk.

Sunday afternoon Emily sat in the living room, watching for Pastor Ben's car. He'd called to ask if he could stop by, and Emily agreed. She wished Marti were here to help her entertain him, but she and Randy were out for the day.

Out for the day. Emily longed to have a life where she could be "out for the day." Since Greg had telephoned Thursday morning, she'd struggled with her thoughts. He sounded distracted...almost as if he had more to say but had stopped himself. She wanted to read between the lines, but nothing made sense.

Fear weighed against her chest, while she was thinking about Greg's words on the telephone. "We have to talk when I come back."

The words froze in her heart. She had almost allowed herself to fall in love. Almost? If reality didn't hurt so badly, she would laugh. She *had* fallen in love—that was the problem. She'd slowly begun to trust again, and once more, she felt betrayed.

And now, what could she say to Pastor Ben? He was a good man, encouraging her to lay her burdens at Jesus' feet. How she longed to do that. But something was wrong with her. She wasn't worthy. She felt as if God had turned His back on her, and she didn't know why.

Tears pressed against her eyes. As she wiped them away, she heard a car in the driveway. No time to check her makeup. She hoped the pastor wouldn't notice she'd been crying.

She eased her way to the foyer, and when he rang the bell, Emily opened the door. The August sun shimmered heat waves on the cement, and Emily encouraged him to hurry inside so she could close the door against the hot air.

"You're looking very good, Emily."

"Thank you. Would you like something cold to drink? Iced tea or lemonade?

"Lemonade would be great. Thanks." He followed her into the kitchen, and once she poured the beverages, he carried them to the living room.

"Thanks," she said when he set her drink on the table. Emily motioned to the sofa. "Please, have a seat."

He sat where she'd suggested, and Emily released her walker and sank into the recliner across from him. She pulled the lever to elevate her legs.

"So tell me how thing are going," he said.

Without inclination, tears returned to her eyes and she let them fall, tired of fighting her emotions.

Without pressing for an explanation, Pastor Ben waited. When she had calmed, he handed her his handkerchief. "When you're ready, I'd be happy to listen," he said. That was all.

He leaned back, propping an ankle on the opposite knee and folded his hands in his lap.

Emily stared at him, not knowing what to say. She'd said it all before. Or had she? The thoughts piled in her head like Pick Up sticks.

"I don't know where to begin…if I wanted to," she said.

"The old cliché says to start at the beginning. What's the first thought that pops into your head?"

"Greg" shot from her mouth before she could stop herself.

"Greg?" A quizzical expression settled on his face. "What about Greg?"

"I don't want to love him."

"But you do?"

She nodded, her pulse racing with her admission.

"Why don't you want to love him, Emily?" He lowered his leg and leaned forward with folded hands, resting his elbows on his knees.

A myriad of thoughts tumbled through her mind. Because Greg should be a father. Because Greg deserved better. Because...

"Can you tell me?" he asked.

Emily shrugged, brushing the tears from her eyes. "Because he doesn't love me."

"Are you—"

"He says he cares about me."

His eyes narrowed. "But you don't think he does?"

"No. He cares, but he cares about everyone. He's active with the Special Olympics. You should see the love in his eyes for those children. He cares about his patients. But I want more than caring. I don't think he loves me."

"Why would you think that?"

"I don't know." She sorted her reasons. "His actions differ from what he says."

Pastor Ben dragged his fingers through his hair. "You mean he says he cares for you, but he doesn't show it?"

"Yes...well...no. Not exactly."

His frown deepened, and so did hers.

"You see, I'm confused. He's done so many things for me. Wonderful things."

"Wonderful things?"

Greg's kindnesses settled in her thoughts. "He cleaned out my flower beds and planted my garden. He brought me a huge floral arrangement when I was in the hospital. When he disappointed me because he had to work overtime at the hospital, he came the next evening with his arms filled the groceries and cooked my dinner."

The visions bounced into her thoughts like popcorn in hot oil. "So many things like that."

Then Greg's telephone call came to mind. "He telephoned from the airport Thursday before he left for his conference."

The pastor rose and flexed his shoulders, then ambled across the room before turning back to Emily. "What do you expect from him, Emily? How has he disappointed you?"

Silence flooded the room. What did she expect? Had she been truthful with Pastor Ben? She wanted Greg to love her, but more, she feared that she would disappoint him.

"I don't know," she said, unable to look him in the eye.

"I think you do."

"But they're foolish things. Unimportant. I'm ashamed of myself."

He strode to her side. "Never be ashamed, not when you're being honest. The solution to many problems is communication. Maybe you haven't been open with Greg."

"Before he left for Denver, he said we needed to talk," she said.

Pastor rested his hand on her shoulder. "Then that's a start."

"But he didn't kiss me goodbye." She could only whisper the words.

Then silence.

"It's foolish things like that," she continued. "I question every nuance. I try to second-guess every vocal inflection, looking for innuendoes. I ask myself if God is punishing me because I'd lost my trust in Him."

She let the words spill out, piling one on top of the other, like the same Pick Up sticks, but this time, she didn't have to pull them out one by one. They were all there on the table for the pastor to sort.

"Then it's not Greg but God you still don't trust."

The weight of his words fell on her shoulders. She cringed with the awareness.

"We talked before, Emily. I think you're punishing yourself because you cannot imagine a God who is totally forgiving. One who holds you in His heart while you're struggling to be free. One who numbers each hair on your head because you're so precious to Him."

Comprehending, she sat frozen. Everything he said had been true. She couldn't imagine a God who could love so completely.

"You can't punish yourself enough to earn forgiveness, Emily. It's free. God gave us His Son. You know this. Only you've filled your mind with so many fears, there's no room for truth."

He lifted his hand from her shoulder and returned to the sofa. "You can't solve all your problems alone. And I really don't think you want to."

Tears rolled down Emily's cheeks. "I'm tired of being alone. I want to be loved. I want to live again...." Once more, the Easter banners filled her thoughts. From death to life. She'd been dead for so long that now she feared life.

She closed her eyes and opened them again, refocusing on Pastor Ben. "I don't know if I can handle rejection. I fear that if I love Greg with all my heart—and I already do—that he'll be taken from me." Or leave me because I can't have children. Her conscience screamed in her head.

The sobs tore from her chest, pouring out into the afternoon sunlight. She'd said the words she'd hidden even from herself. She'd let them fly into the air, too late to hold them back.

Chapter Nine

Emily grinned, amazed at how good she felt today. Her therapy had gone well, her legs stronger. Soon she'd be walking with the cane. Being free from the chair and walker pumped her spirit.

But it wasn't only her legs that cheered her. After the pastor left Sunday afternoon, she'd had a heart-to-heart talk with herself. Everything Pastor Ben had said was true and her own attitude was all that kept her from being the person she wanted to be. If God's will brought her and Greg together, God would solve her problems and calm her fears.

And children? That problem sat like a weight on her soul, but she prayed the Lord would give her wisdom. He would guide her when the time came to do what was best.

She watched the physical therapist climb into his car. Then hearing the telephone ring, she turned and made her way to the kitchen.

When she answered, happiness permeated her voice.

"Emily?"

Greg. Her heart dipped to her stomach. She swallowed

back her old ways and tugged out her new confidence. "Hi, you're back."

"Yes, late last night. You sound wonderful."

"I do?" She shrugged. "I guess, I do. My *other* physical therapist just left. He makes me laugh."

Kicking herself, she'd already ruined her new resolve. *Lord, keep me focused on trust and give me confidence.*

"I thought of you so much while I was gone," he said. "But let's not talk about that. I'm back now—hear the drum roll—and I'm not going anywhere…at least in the near future."

She pushed away the negative thoughts slithering into her mind—like why shouldn't we talk about it or what do you mean by the "near future"? She hated those prodding questions.

"I'm glad, Greg." Pleased, she knew she'd given an honest response. Being truthful about her feelings took too much work…and left her open for hurt. But she wanted to stick to her self-made promise and keep her mind focused on God's assurance.

"How's your physical therapy going?" Greg asked.

"He tells me I'm doing wonderfully. Almost ready to jog."

Greg's chuckle rippled over the line. "Do I hear a touch of sarcasm in your voice?"

"Just a smidgeon."

"I can handle a smidgeon."

His voice sounded lighthearted and she could imagine his dimple flickering as he spoke. She pictured him in his white smock with the hospital logo on the pocket, his broad shoulders and ready smile warming her heart.

"I'm coming to see you later," he said, though he faltered as if waiting for her response.

"Okay," she said.

Emily kicked herself for not saying she was thrilled or

she couldn't wait. "I'm anxious to see you." She felt better saying it.

"I'm glad, Em. I'll see you about six and don't eat. I'm
bringing dinner for all of us."

"All of us? Are you bringing friends?"

A light chuckle struck her ear. "I meant for Marti, too."

"She's busy tonight."

"Okay. So it'll be an intimate dinner for two." His
voice sounded warm.

"I can't wait," she murmured, speaking from her heart.

Greg appraised the safety of the paper bags propped on
the passenger seat, pleased that they were still standing.
The aroma filled the car, and if the food tasted half as
good as it smelled, he'd be happy.

He'd never tried gourmet carryout before. Emily would
be surprised. She'd most likely expect him to arrive with
pizza or burgers. But he wanted something special for tonight.

In Denver, Greg had spent many hours trying to sleep
but instead thought about Emily and their situation. He
loved her. He'd settled on that fact before his airplane had
left Detroit Metro Airport. The other dilemma—never having children—still left an ache in his chest, but he'd agreed
to put it in God's hands.

Who was he to question God? Who was that doctor who
made the prognosis? What right did either of them have
to predict the future? From the moment he'd faced that,
Greg's spirit had lifted and his decision had been made.

In her driveway, he gathered the two sacks in his arms
and headed for the porch, his pulse surging. Tonight he
wanted to be open and honest with Emily…if he could
rouse his courage.

She greeted him at the door with a smile, and her expression shifted to surprise when she saw the bags. "No pizza?"

"I hope you're not disappointed?" He slid an arm around her waist and brushed his lips against hers.

Her face brightened. "Not a bit." She tilted her head, trying to read the black script emblazoned across the silver paper. "What's that say?"

"Go Gourmet." He chuckled at the logo. "One of my co-workers said it's great food."

"Sounds interesting." She arched a teasing brow, pushed the door closed and headed down the hall toward the kitchen. "Look how fast I'm walking."

"Whoa! Hold it," he said. "You wait in the living room. When I'm ready, I'll call you."

She did a double take and turned the walker around toward the wide archway. "Yes, sir, Mr. P.T."

Her voice rang with an easy warmth. The sensation settled in his chest, expanding to joy. What had happened while he was gone? He sure wouldn't ask. No sense in ruining the blessed miracle.

Standing in the kitchen, he eyed the cabinets and drawers. He found white table linen in her pantry, snatched out a crystal candle holder and spotted a package of pale yellow candles.

He set the table with Emily's best china, then stood back, amazed he had created an attractive table setting alone. He'd noticed a radio on the kitchen counter and snapped it on, then found a gentle jazz station. He gave a final look. A view. Pushing back the curtains, he brought the late-afternoon garden into view.

Within moments, he'd warmed the entrée and garnished the plate with sprigs of rosemary, lit the candle, then snapped off the light and headed for the living room.

As he stepped through the archway, she greeted him

with a sweet grin. He beckoned, and she boosted herself from the chair and met him in the doorway.

"It's great to see your eyes sparkle. You're a lovely woman, Em."

A pale flush colored her cheeks, and she tilted her head shyly. "Thanks. You're pretty handsome yourself."

"I bet you say that to all the men," he said, echoing her typical response. "I missed you."

"I missed you, too."

Thrilled with her breathy admission, his stomach tightened. She'd opened her heart and said the words he'd longed to hear.

Resting his palm against her cheek, Greg noted a faint tremor. He yearned to kiss her until he couldn't breathe, but he controlled the racing emotions. Emily needed tenderness and assurance. She needed to trust again—both him and God—and he had promised himself to move slowly.

"We'd better eat before dinner gets cold," he said, brushing a kiss across her lips.

She released a sweet sigh and walked ahead of him down the hallway. She hesitated when she reached the kitchen and gazed at him over her shoulder. "Greg, you found everything. I can't believe it. It's so pretty." She faced him with a chuckle. "I'm not sure I could remember where the candlesticks were."

"It's amazing what a person can do when they're determined." His thought moved with swift transition to her knees. She'd clung to her wheelchair with incredible determination. Now he prayed she would be as persistent about walking…and loving again.

She used the table and his arm for support as she settled into the chair. He joined her and clasped both her hands for the blessing. When he raised his eyes, he caught a glint of moisture on her lashes.

Bewildered, he studied her. "Are you okay?"

With a speedy swipe of a freed hand, she brushed the tears away. "I'm more than okay, Greg. I'm touched."

"Because I brought you carryout?"

"Because you're so thoughtful and you made everything so pretty."

He caressed her hand. "It looks wonderful on you."

"My tears?" Her face twisted to a silly smile.

"Not your tears, but your frankness. Your honesty."

With his hand still in hers, Emily lifted it to her lips and pressed a kiss against his fingers.

Warmth radiated up his arm and blanketed his heart. His own tears pushed behind his eyes, and he sensed God's loving presence surrounding them.

Emily shifted her attention to her plate, drawing in a lengthy whiff of the tempting meal. "It smells delicious and even looks as good." She slivered a piece of the meat and slid it between her lips. She savored the flavor. "Luscious."

He plied his fork and tasted the creamy potato concoction. "It is," he agreed.

"Should I ask what I'm eating?"

"I couldn't pronounce it if I wanted to." He recalled the French titles that the clerk had to translate into English. "Chicken with rosemary and chives, potatoes in some kind of cheese sauce, white asparagus with...only heaven can remember what, and herbed bread. And don't ask which herbs."

She clasped his hand. "And my best china, white table linen, candlelight, music and you."

The glowing flame shimmered across her fair skin and glints of gold flickered in her copper-colored hair. He had prayed all the while he was in Denver that tonight would be like this...that the cocoon that bound Emily's life for so long would open and the love she'd kept wrapped in silken threads would come to life again.

His gaze drifted from her fiery tresses to the colorful garden glimmering in the rays of the setting sun. Everything was perfect except...

His promise. He released a ragged breath. He'd promised to tell her about Aaron.

Emily gazed across the candlelight. Though disturbed by her nagging feelings, she longed to give her heart free rein. For too long she'd tethered her emotions with anger and guilt. With new knees she could walk again, pain-free, and if Greg truly cared for her, she could love again, guilt-free. Children? Could she leave that problem to God? She ached with her question.

From the corner of her eye, colors glinted from the yard, not only flowers, but the sunset sky spread with all the spectrums of the rainbow. God's natural paint box.

A final thought edged to her heart. With a new perspective and her growing love for Greg, she could fully love the Lord again. The thought eased her mind, and peace spread through her as warm and lovely as the setting sun painted across the heavens.

"You're quiet," Greg said, ending the silence.

"Just thinking. Thanking God for the glorious sunset." She slid her hand across the table and touched his arm. "And for you."

"Emily, I've wanted to hear you say that for so long." He pressed his hand against hers. "And without holding back. Being with you feels good and comfortable."

"I know." Good and comfortable. His words were hers. The rich sensation of contentment and peace eased down her back and through her limbs. For a moment, even her knees felt as if they were her own.

"Would you do something for me?" Greg asked.

The tone of his voice coaxed her to agree. "What?"

"Walk with me in the garden."

"Walk? Me?"

"With your walker. But it won't be long, Emily. A couple more weeks, and you'll be using the cane."

"You think?"

"I know."

A mixture of anxiety and hope flooded her thoughts. She wouldn't rush. When she felt steady and secure, then she would use her cane. But now, he'd asked her to walk with him in the dusky evening. "I will if you'll help me down the back steps."

He rose and offered his arm to help her stand. She pulled the walker toward her, and they moved to the doorway. Greg opened the door wide and held it back until she was on the porch. Then she took one step at a time to the grass.

Through the tree branches, a wash of gold and coral rested on the lilac horizon. With caution, she measured each step across the grass until they had reached the pathway. The fragrance of roses hung on the air. The last rays warmed her bare arms.

Greg ambled beside her, not hurrying, but moving in her slower gait. They talked about the gardens and his trip to Denver. Conversation about everyday things floated into the air and cushioned in her chest like coming home.

In the middle of the flower-bordered path, a butterfly flitted past and rested on a faded purple coneflower. Its wings paused a moment, the dusty design yellow and brown against the grayish petal. Her memory drew back to Easter and the butterfly banners reminding her of the rebirth and resurrection.

Emily's gaze sought Greg's. He took her hands in his. In silence he searched her face. But for once, she didn't fear his quiet demeanor. She felt as she hoped he did— companionship and oneness.

"On the phone, you mentioned that when you come home we would talk, and it made me think. While you were away, I did a lot of soul-searching myself." Hiding her nervousness, she directed her gaze to his. "I'd like to tell you about it."

Chapter Ten

Greg's expression wavered with confusion. "Is something wrong, Em?"

"No. Not really." Emily braved her apprehension. "Pastor Ben came by, and I talked about a lot of feelings and fears I'd never faced before."

The confusion faded and a new look rose to his face. "I was ready to say the same thing to you. While I was in Denver, I struggled with a few things myself."

Her stomach tightened. "What kind of things?"

"Nothing that affects us, Em. It's about me, things I've never told anyone."

"Things you've never to—"

"Please, don't worry." He motioned to the garden bench. "First tell me what you thought about while I was gone."

Emily lowered herself to the wooden slats, curiosity niggling in her mind, yet determination propelled her. She had to tell him what she discovered about herself.

Greg sat at her side, his fingers gripping the edge of the bench seat.

"You already know a lot of this," Emily began. "We've talked about the grief I felt over Ted's death and my frustration that God didn't answer my prayers."

He didn't speak, but gave a single nod.

"As I thought about our relationship, ready to toss it off as a bad effort, I realized that I was taking my frustration out on you. The truth is, I was angry at myself. Angry for expecting miracles and having God respond with His will and not mine."

"It's not easy."

"It isn't. But most of all, I think that I've felt unworthy all this time. I called it God's betrayal, but I felt I was being punished. Retribution for my unforgiving heart. And I transferred my frustration to our relationship."

"You thought I was punishing you?"

"Punishment, no. I gave God all the credit for that. But, Greg, I was punishing myself. And my greatest fear was…" She faltered as tears rose to her eyes and rolled to her cheeks.

"What, Em?" He captured her hands in his.

"My greatest fear was that I would love again and God would take that love away."

"You mean you were afraid I might die?"

"That…or you really didn't love me at all."

"But—"

"Or that you might stop loving me. I know how wonderful you've been, but I guess deep inside I feared you might be acting out of pity."

"*Pity?* Emily, I've never…" He paused and closed his eyes for a moment. Honesty, he reminded himself. "Maybe at the beginning I was saddened by your life in that chair. I couldn't bear to think that's how you'd spend your life when it wasn't necessary. But not pity, frustration that you would choose to stay there. But it only took minutes before I loved you."

"I realize that now, Greg. I was pushing you away before you pushed me away. Snapping at you, making snide remarks, thinking ridiculous things. But then I faced what was really happening.''

She paused, searching his face and wishing she could tell him the rest. But she'd said enough. It was his turn to talk. ''That's all I wanted to say.''

For a long time his eyes searched hers. ''Are you sure?''

The question sifted into her consciousness, but she could tell him no more now. And the look in Greg's eyes said he needed to tell her what was on his mind. ''I'm sure.''

Greg studied the look of curiosity on Emily's face. He didn't want to ruin the special night with his admission, but if they were speaking from their hearts, he had no choice.

''I'm glad you told me what you've been through, Em. Because something happened when I was young that I've hidden from everyone…even my mom. I promised myself, I'd get it off my chest. So here goes.''

He drew in a long, deep breath. ''I don't know if I've told you why I became a physical therapist.''

She shook her head, her eyes filled with concern.

He rested his elbows on his knees and knitted his fingers together. ''I wanted a job helping people keep whole, healthy bodies. To help damaged limbs become strong. I wanted to be a part of helping someone walk again.''

''It's your gift, Greg.''

He grimaced. ''A gift for some, but for me it was penance.''

''Penance?''

''A self-punishment for my sin.'' His heart thundered and throbbed in his temple. ''I wasn't an only child, Emily. I had a younger brother, Aaron.''

Emily's eyes darted to his. ''What happened?''

''He died. And I—I've spent my life feeling responsible.''

''Oh, Greg.'' She caught his hands in hers. ''But why?''

''Like all little brothers, I loved him, but he was a pain. Whatever I did, he wanted to do the same whether he was old enough or not. He died one winter during a sledding accident.''

Greg swallowed to control the rising emotion that knotted his throat and tore at his heart.

''I loved to sled on the hills near my house, but one, in particular, was too dangerous. At the bottom was the highway. But I'd taken chances and learned to control the sled. On that day, Aaron followed me up the hill, whining that he wanted to go sledding, too. I took him down some small hills, then told him to wait while I rode down the other.''

''But he wanted to go with you,'' Emily said.

He nodded. ''He bugged me until I agreed. 'Only once,' I said. 'Then I'll go down alone.' I'd planned to overturn the sled before we reached the bottom.'' He kneaded the tension knotting in his neck. ''You can imagine what happened.''

''Was it a car or...'' She paused, then studied him. ''Were you hurt, too, Greg?''

''I tilted the sled and fell off, but Aaron didn't. The sled flew down the hill and he had no idea how to control it. It shot out into the highway and...''

Greg covered his face with his hands. ''I can still see the cars swerve and hear the crash,'' he whispered.

Weighted silence hung on the air. Emily sat unmoving, except for her thumb caressing his fingers.

''Aaron's legs and pelvis were crushed. He lived only a few hours. My parents assumed he took the sled without asking, and I could never tell them the truth.''

She lifted his hand and kissed his fingers. ''But what is the truth, Greg? You see one truth, but what would the world see?''

Confused, he shook his head. ''I don't know, Em.''

''You see an older brother who should have been more careful—who should have known better and said no. But what do I see?''

He could only shrug, sorting out what she was saying.

''I see a boy who loved his kid brother so much that he

couldn't say no. Even adults dote on their kids, not always with their best interest at heart. You loved your brother, so you agreed out of love, not out of common sense. And a child's common sense on top of everything."

"I've tried to convince myself of that, but I die a little inside every time I think about it."

"It's natural. But not because of your guilt, but because of your loss."

"But why does God allow those things to happen? No matter how hard I try to understand, I never will."

"We can't understand. We're not God. The Father sees the bigger plan. Would you have become a therapist if that accident hadn't happened?"

He lifted a shoulder. "I don't know. I wanted to be a truck driver." He managed a faint smile. "I liked science, but I probably would have gone into engineering or something."

"And now, have you helped people use their arms? Have you taught injured children to walk again? Have you given people with little hope a new life?"

"You know the answer."

"Then could that be God's plan for you?"

"But did he have to take my little brother?"

"What did life have in store for Aaron? We'll never know. But God knows."

A ragged sigh shuddered through him. Emily was right. He didn't know. Only God knew. And, he supposed, that was enough.

"I'm not saying you won't grieve," Emily said, "or that you won't feel guilty you lived and Aaron died. But I think God takes charge to save us from something worse."

She paused, rubbing her fingers across her forehead. "I suppose it's the same with Ted's death. I've not been able to understand that, either. And here I am explaining the same thing to you."

Greg slid his arm around her shoulders and nestled her

to his side. In time, even if they didn't fully understand, they might both come to accept God's will in their lives.

Emily stood beneath the glorious leaves, taking in the myriad of color and the crisp scent of autumn. "Thanks for suggesting this, Greg. It's a beautiful way to spend a Sunday."

With a quiet chuckle, Greg rested his hand on her shoulder. "And look at you. Can you believe it? Walking in the park."

She lifted the hand-carved cane he'd given her. "Walking with this, but closer every day to doing it on my own."

A scarlet leaf drifted on the breeze and caught in Emily's hair. She raised her hand and withdrew it from her tresses. "Pretty," she said, showing it to Greg. "A sugar maple."

"Pretty, maybe, but not as beautiful as you." He curved his arm around her waist, and they ambled toward the picnic tables under the sun-kissed trees.

When she sank to the bench, a contented sigh left her. "Could anything be more perfect?" She laid her cane on the rough-hewn table and patted her knees. "Even these things are beginning to feel as if they belong to me."

"And where would you be without them?"

She shook her head. "In my chair." She turned to him. "God has the most wonderful way of fixing things. I had expected the worst and I got the best. You."

He brushed her cheek with his finger. "Look at the color in your cheeks and your smile. My life is as close to perfect as it can get without being in heaven."

Her pulse skipped then galloped along her limbs, remembering the one thing she hadn't talked about. She lifted her eyes to his, wanting so badly to tell him that she may never have children. Her shoulders slumped at the thought. He'd never mentioned marriage so she'd soothed herself with his precious friendship, knowing the horrible prognosis could remain unspoken.

"Sad?" Greg asked, a scowl growing on his face.

"No. Why?" She straightened her spine, realizing her mood had taken a downward spiral. "I guess my thoughts slid back to my time spent in that wheelchair. It's hard to believe I wanted to stay there."

"People are willing to stick with what they know, because the unknown scares them."

"I was so afraid I'd go through the surgery and end up worse than I was." A sad chuckle left her. "But what could have been worse? I suppose lots of things, but I don't want to think about them."

Greg ran his hand across her back and slid his fingers to her hairline, caressing the nape of her neck.

"I know. I lived with Aaron's accident for so long, and since I told you about it that day, a peace settled over me I never thought I'd feel again. Sometimes just telling someone helps. But lately, Em, the good feeling isn't sitting as well."

"Why?" She observed his growing frown.

"Because the other person I should've told is my mother."

She nodded. "How do you think she'd take it?"

"I don't know." He closed his eyes. "I really don't. We've been close, and I suppose that's why. Without admitting my part in the accident, I've tried to make up for Aaron's death."

He was silent for a long time.

"I don't know how she'd feel or what she'd say," he said finally.

"You need to tell her, Greg. It'll make everything right."

"It took so much courage to tell you...I wonder if I can."

"Why did you tell me?"

He touched her chin, drawing his finger along her lower lip. "You don't know?" He looked deeply into her eyes. "Because I love you, Em. That horrible experience affected my life. It made me who I am with all my fears and idiosyncrasies, with all my drives and motivation. I want to spend my life with you. And…I needed to tell you.''

Her breathing faltered and she swallowed a gasp. I want to spend my life with you. She'd sensed it, but he'd never said it. The reality caught in her throat. If he asked her to marry him, she had to refuse. No matter what he said, she had to say no.

''I needed your forgiveness and understanding,'' he continued. ''Now I need my mom's.''

''Greg, there's nothing to forgive. I told you the day in the garden. You've suffered too long for a child's mistake. A misjudgment based on love. No one could be angry at you for that. No one.''

She'd suffered, too, with her fear of never having a child. Would Greg forgive her for not telling him? For not stopping him from loving her?

In the hush of the afternoon, she turned her eyes to the heavens. Autumn hues splashed the dying foliage, and tears rose in her eyes, blurring the landscape while the burnished leaves flowed together like watercolors on a sky-blue background.

Chapter Eleven

Sitting in his mother's kitchen, Greg stared through the patio door at her fading garden. Only the hardy mums stood in round bunches adding a splotch of bright color to the brown crispy leaves of the dead plants.

Rose set two teacups on the table. The spicy orange fragrance curled up from the hot liquid.

"Smells good," Greg said, pulling his gaze from the flower beds.

"Something's on your mind."

Her words were not a question, but a statement, and despite his discomfort, Greg felt a grin tug at his mouth. "You're like Solomon, Mom. You seem to know everything."

"Just a mother's instinct...and your face. It reads like a book." A faint frown appeared. "You're not having a problem with Emily?"

He gave her a real grin this time. "It's not Emily. She's fine. Her knees improve a little more each day. She'll be walking outside without the cane in another week or so."

"That's grand. She's a wonderful woman, Greg. The kind of girl a mother dreams her son will marry."

He raised his downcast eyes to her. "Now, why doesn't that surprise me?"

"Maybe it's a son's instinct," she said, giving him a pat. "But this isn't getting to the problem."

Greg turned his head to the window again, closed his eyes and whispered a prayer. "I feel like a child, trying to tell you about some terrible thing I did."

"You're not a child. But I loved you then, and I love you now. Whatever it is, I'll understand."

"I hope you will. This has been a burden since I was a kid." He caught her gaze and held it.

His mother frowned, but didn't blink an eye. Her silence pressed against Greg's chest, limiting his breath.

"Since you were a child? That's a long time to hang on to a problem…and unnecessarily. Your dad and I were never angry at you for long."

"No, you weren't." He found his courage and began. "It's about Aaron's death, Mom…how it happened. You never knew the full story."

Her face twisted with sorrow. "But I guessed, Greg."

His chest tightened. "What do you mean?"

"Your dad and I thought there was more to the story. I could see it in your face." Slowly fear rose in her eyes. "It was an accident?"

Greg's hand grasped his mother's arm. "Yes, Mom. It was an accident, but I felt so responsible."

Tears filled her eyes. She pressed her palm against his hand. "Then tell me what really happened."

Greg told her the story from the moment Aaron followed him up the hill to the horrendous collision at the bottom. Tears puddled in his eyes and he pushed them away with the back of his hand. "I felt so responsible."

Rose wiped away her own tears. "I'm sure you did. You

were Aaron's older brother. Your dad and I always told you to watch out for him. Parents do that. The older takes care of the younger. I'm so sorry you didn't tell us.'' Her sad eyes searched his.

"Fear. I thought you'd hate me.''

"Hate you? Oh, Greg—''

"I should have been firm with Aaron. But I gave in, then I thought God made me pay for it when he died.''

Rose wagged her head, her eyes downcast. "No, Greg. Aaron's death wasn't God's payback. It was His will.''

"His will? Why?''

"We'll never know. But the Lord is loving, not vindictive.''

Greg couldn't find the words to speak, but hung his head, staring at the table. "I was so angry that God hadn't let me die instead of Aaron.'' The memories crashed into his thoughts. He recalled being alone in the night, crying and bargaining with the Lord to bring Aaron back and to take him instead.

"I wish you'd told us. We could have helped you. Your dad and I could never hate you.''

"But a child doesn't use common sense.''

"That's true. You thought you were guilty.'' She drew in a deep breath. "You loved Aaron, Greg. And you've tried to make restitution for his death. I can see that now.'' Her gaze drifted through the window to the garden. "I wonder if you'd been a physical therapist if that hadn't happened.''

Greg's eyes widened. "Funny you say that. Emily asked the same thing.''

"I'm glad you told Emily.'' Rose lifted her cup and sipped the tea. "You've helped people walk without pain and brought smiles to frightened faces. If you could buy your way to heaven, Greg, you've made a valiant effort.''

Filled with remorse, he pushed a halfhearted grin to his

face. "It took a while, but I realize that God's forgiven me. But I need to know that you forgive me, too, Mom. Then maybe I can forgive myself."

"There is no need for forgiveness. You were blameless. Aaron was a terrible nag, but as cute as a bug's ear. I gave in to him many times when I shouldn't have. I'm as guilty as you." Tears pooled again in her eyes. "If he'd learned that no meant no, you wouldn't have had a problem."

"Let's not dredge up more blame or guilt. I needed to get this off my chest. I feel better."

"And wholly forgiven, Greg. By God and by me...and, I pray, yourself."

His mother's message flowed into his thoughts like a quiet, gentle stream. He relaxed his tense shoulders and leaned against the chair back. Eyeing the tea, he lifted the cup to his lips. "Cold." He gave her a wry grin.

She stood and carried his cup to the microwave. They waited in silence while the teacup twirled behind the glass door. When the buzzer sounded, she carried the steaming cup back to the table.

"Thanks," he said. "And thanks for understanding."

"I'm your mother." With a faint smile, she ran her finger around the edge of her drink. "Now, let's get down to business."

Greg's head shot upward. "Business?"

"Emily," she said. "Are you going to marry this woman or not?"

Greg threw his head back and laughed. "You and Shakespeare, Mom. You sure know when someone needs comic relief."

Her brow wrinkled as she eyed him. "I didn't think that was funny. I'm serious. I think you've found a soul mate, Greg. A beautiful Christian woman and about your age. And if you two hurry, you might even give me a grandchild or two before I die."

A jolt of deep sorrow struck him, but he couldn't speak of that now. He shook his head, rubbing the back of his neck. "You're planning my life right down to the nth degree."

"You haven't found yourself a wife so I'm willing to help."

"I think this is one thing you'll have to leave up to me, Mom."

She left her chair and wrapped her arms around Greg's shoulders. "Do you mean what I think you mean? When? When will you ask her?"

He lifted an eyebrow. "All you're getting from me is name, rank and serial number."

Greg paced in front of the wide door leading to the Venetian Club's ballroom. When he tired, he took a break and leaned against the wall, waiting for the bride and groom's arrival while envisioning Emily in the long green gown. Wedding photographs took forever.

Greg had been awed by Emily's loveliness as she walked unaided down the long, church aisle. She'd been so busy with her matron-of-honor responsibilities, Greg hadn't had time to tell her how beautiful she looked.

Applause echoed across the room and halted the noisy conversation. Greg turned toward the ballroom's double doors. When Emily entered, he caught his breath and signaled to her.

She spotted him and headed his way. "Finally." She released a sigh. "I thought the photographer would never stop." She brushed his cheek with her fingers. "I missed you."

He drew her to him. "That dress looks good on you, Em. You look beautiful."

"Thanks." Her face etched with concern. "You mean I didn't resemble a Christmas tree?"

He chuckled. "No. You looked gorgeous, and I felt so good seeing you walk all the way down the aisle."

"I was so afraid everyone could tell I had artificial knees."

"They'd only notice that if you'd been carrying the X rays."

She laughed and pulled a playful punch to his upper arm.

He nuzzled her hair.

"I thought Marti looked radiant," Emily said.

"She did, but my eyes were only on you."

She clasped his arm. "Did you notice how nervous I was? You'd think it had been my own wedding."

Her own wedding. Had she read his mind? He wiped the thought away. "I'll get some punch before we sit."

She nodded, and he filled two glasses, then headed toward their seats.

After the meal was served, Greg led Emily from the ballroom. They followed a wide hallway leading to a quiet atrium. Ferns and hanging plants filled the room, and stone benches nestled amid the greenery along the glass windows.

"Let's sit," Greg said, looking out at the pines and bare-limbed trees bordering the stretch of lawn. He gestured to the bench.

She raised a cautious eye to his. "But not too long, Greg. Marti'll wonder where I am."

"Just for a few minutes."

She nodded and sank to the seat, facing the window.

During the afternoon, the gray sky hung heavy with clouds, brightened only by an occasional glint of hazy sun. But as they watched, the evening's cold had opened the clouds, and white flakes drifted on the winter wind and clung to the dried limbs.

He nestled her in his arms as they watched the snow accumulate on the bare limbs shrouding them in white.

"It'll be a real white Christmas," Emily said.

"It will."

"So beautiful."

Greg nodded. The building's outdoor spotlights made shimmering circles on the ground, and fragile flakes danced in the silvery rays. Though the setting was beautiful, Greg's gaze soon turned to Emily's face, glowing in the dim light. He slid his hand in hers, wondering how to begin.

"Are you enjoying the wedding?" he asked.

"Yes, but I'd have preferred to spend the whole time with you." She shrugged. "But this was important to Marti and how could I refuse? She was so good to me when I needed her."

"She's your sister, Em." His leg trembled as he fumbled for courage. "Is this the kind of wedding you've dreamed about?" He'd said it. His breath rattled from his constricted chest.

She faced him. "Why?" A frown flashed across her face.

"I'd hoped you might smile at the question, Em."

Ashamed of herself, Emily forced the scowl from her face. "I'm sorry. You surprised me." She rallied her thoughts, wondering why he asked and praying it wasn't what she'd feared. "I really haven't given a wedding much thought. I figured I was too old for marriage now."

"Too old? You're only thirty-five."

"Thirty-six in another month."

"Some people marry late in life and widows often marry again."

He searched her face, and she sensed his anxiety. Apprehension filled her. Was he going to ask her to be his wife? Why hadn't she told him the truth so long ago before they'd fallen in love? She'd been a fool to let it go on this long.

"I—I suppose I...never considered marrying again. I had too many problems to even consider the possibility."

"But not anymore, Em. You're walking and—"

"But that's not the only problem, Greg." Her heart hammered against her chest.

"Em, I can't imagine a problem that you and I couldn't face together."

Tremors rose in her limbs. She knew the truth would have to be shared. She could no longer hide behind her damaged knees.

He slipped his hand into his inside breast pocket, then dropped his fist to his lap. "You know that I want to marry you. I hoped today you'd picture another wedding. Yours and mine. Probably not the white dress and tuxedo, but a beautiful wedding all the same because it would be ours. Didn't that enter your mind at all?"

Overcome by his question, Emily managed a calming breath. She had to tell him the truth...about everything. "Yes. I've imagined us married. Not only today, but many times. But I knew it wasn't going to happen."

Greg clutched her arms and turned her to face him. "Why? I love you, Em, and I'm positive you love me."

Before she realized what he'd done, Greg had placed a small velvet box into her hand. She gazed at the delicate case, and tears rolled from her eyes, dripping to her hands. She had no right to open the gift.

She lifted her misty eyes to the pure white flakes falling outside the window and remembered the doctor's prognosis...the unaltered truth she'd buried so long ago.

"I do love you, Greg, and if I were to marry, you would be my only choice. You're wonderful in every way. But I can't marry anyone."

"Em, please—"

"Let me finish."

She brushed tears from her eyes, praying to stay coherent until she finished what she had to say. "You deserve a whole wife, Greg. A woman who can give you a family. More was injured during that accident than my legs. It's doubtful I can have children."

Greg didn't speak, but brushed away her tears with his fingertips. He lifted her shaking hands to his lips and kissed them. "Em, listen. I have two things to tell you." He gazed lovingly into her eyes.

"What?" His look was unfazed. His staunch demeanor threw her thoughts off balance. She searched his face for a hint. "What things?"

"First—and please don't be upset—Marti told me a long time ago about the doctor's prognosis."

Her fist rose to her chest and a gasp tumbled from her mouth. "But you never said—"

"Marti probably didn't realize when she began that I didn't know, and back then, we'd just begun to fall in love. After I thought about what Marti told me, I struggled with the possibility of not having children, but I love you, and then I realized your prognosis was one doctor's prediction. Not a fact."

She opened her mouth to respond, but he pressed his finger against her lips.

"And the second point—you've forgotten God, Em. If God wants us to be parents, we'll have a child. Medical problems or not. Remember? We can move mountains if we have faith even as small—"

"As a mustard seed," she said with him.

His face spoke volumes—concern, faith, hope and, best of all, the deepest love.

"We'll leave that problem at Jesus' feet," he said. "Children or not, Em, I'm asking you to be my wife. I promise my everlasting love and faithfulness forever."

Her hands trembled as she clutched the velvet box. Her tears, bound by her lashes, misted her sight without leaving a damp trail down her cheeks.

"Open the box, Em," Greg whispered.

With quaking fingers, she lifted the box to her palm and raised the lid. Inside, a cluster of diamonds sparkled with fiery points in the soft light of the atrium. "It's beautiful." She raised her eyes, and her tear-filled gaze glinted as brilliantly as the gems clutched in her hand. "I love you, Greg, with all my heart."

"And?" He waited, searching her face.

"And I'd feel blessed to be your wife."

With his own trembling hand, Greg lifted the ring from the box and slid it onto her finger, then tilted her chin. "I even adore this proud chin of yours. So stubborn and determined."

"And I adore those dimples of yours," she said, pressing her lips against each cheek.

He rose and helped her stand, then entwined their fingers. "You've made my life complete, Em. You've helped me deal with my sorrow and filled my life with so many precious days."

"I can't even remember all the fears that crumbled away," Emily said. "You're strong and determined. My life is whole again, and, God willing, our marriage will be complete...with a family. It's in His hands."

Greg drew Emily to his chest, and she encircled her arms around his neck. When their lips met, joy wrapped around their hearts, binding them together forever.

Chapter Twelve

✥

Summer, three years later

Emily took a deep breath, savoring the sweet floral scent that clung to the air. In the summer sun, her butterfly garden surged with color and fragrance. She snatched the last few determined weeds from the snapdragons, then made her way to the brilliant dahlia beds. For the past two years, she and Rose had traded tubers, and now both gardens blossomed with a profusion of those glorious flowers.

Her mind drifted to a few years earlier when she sat nailed to her wheelchair, refusing to trust. But Greg had changed all that. Not long ago, Pastor Ben had given a sermon on First Peter. She remember the gist of it. Flowers, grass and people die, but God's promises live forever. The verse had given her blessed assurance.

Now, instead of eyeing the overgrown flower beds from the kitchen window, she walked daily along the garden path, free from pain and free from loneliness. God had given her more than she deserved, more than she could have imagined.

"Em."

She turned, hearing Greg's voice.

"Look," he called, pointing to the garden path.

Emily lowered her eyes, and her heart surged with joy.

"Mama." One-year-old Rachel sat on the path, her arms outstretched toward her mother, a butterfly fluttering in her hand.

Emily's heart stood still as Rachel rose on her own and balanced on wobbly legs. The butterfly had long since parted, spreading its colorful wings against the afternoon sky.

Not so long ago Emily had spread her own unbound wings and the trip had been wonderful. From Death to Life. The remembered Easter message filled her heart.

Greg reached Emily's side, grinning like a doting father. Arm in arm, they gazed at God's gift, their lovely daughter. As always, Greg's unyielding trust had been correct. With faith as tiny as a mustard seed, miracles could happen.

Emily's miracle teetered from side to side, then lifted her foot and stepped forward, her eyes wide with surprise.

"Greg, Rachel took her first step," Emily whispered.

Opening her arms, Emily took a step forward, but Greg grasped her and held her back. "Wait," he breathed.

Rachel's copper hair glowed in the sunlight, her small, chubby arms open to them, her face tilted upward with a wide grin.

Emily longed to run to her daughter's outstretched arms, but waited.

Rachel's foot moved again, and she wobbled two steps forward on shaky legs before Greg lost his own battle and scooped her up into his arms.

"She walked, Em."

"And in the garden."

Lifting her arms, Emily encircled the two most precious

people in her life and gazed into their smiling eyes. "Thank you, Father," she whispered.

From the corner of her eye, she spotted a flash of color. She held her breath. A monarch butterfly settled on her shoulder, its wings outstretched...

Like Emily.

*   *   *   *   *

Next Month From Steeple Hill's

A LOVE WORTH WAITING FOR

BY

JILLIAN HART

Handsome jet-setter Noah Ashton was everything small-town schoolteacher Julie Renton had ever hoped for. But even while she opened the jaded tycoon's eyes to the Lord's most precious blessings, she sensed Noah had the power to shatter her fragile heart....

Don't miss

A LOVE WORTH WAITING FOR

On sale March 2003

Take 2 inspirational love stories FREE!

PLUS get a FREE surprise gift!

Mail to Steeple Hill Reader Service™

In U.S.
3010 Walden Ave.
P.O. Box 1867
Buffalo, NY 14240-1867

In Canada
P.O. Box 609
Fort Erie, Ontario
L2A 5X3

YES! Please send me 2 free Love Inspired® novels and my free surprise gift. After receiving them, if I don't wish to receive anymore, I can return the shipping statement marked cancel. If I don't cancel, I will receive 3 brand-new novels every month, before they're available in stores! Bill me at the low price of $3.99 each in the U.S. and $4.49 each in Canada, plus 25¢ shipping and handling and applicable sales tax, if any*. That's the complete price and a saving of over 10% off the cover prices—quite a bargain! I understand that accepting the books and gift places me under no obligation ever to buy any books. I can always return a shipment and cancel at any time. Even if I never buy another book from Steeple Hill, the 2 free books and the surprise gift are mine to keep forever.

103 IDN DNU6
303 IDN DNU7

Name _____ (PLEASE PRINT)

Address _____ Apt. No. _____

City _____ State/Prov. _____ Zip/Postal Code _____